Blood.

Blood everywhere.

Blood dripping from the stretchers and countertops, oozing underneath the surgical steel table, soaking into discarded clothing. Blood pooling in congealed puddles on the tiled floor, soaking into the cracks and crevices. Blood spray lining the walls and even the ceiling. Blood splattering the fluorescent lighting.

And in the middle of it all, two bodies. Lifeless, hanging off the beds they lay on, eyes wide open and staring into space. These were once two living things that moved and breathed, and now they are dead.

"Time of death, 0302. Got that? OK, call the morgue and housekeeping. I'll deal with the family. They're in the family room, right? Shit, I hate this part of my job. Anybody want to earn a fast $50? I'll let you borrow my lab coat."

"Fuck that, cowboy. That's why you get paid the big bucks." Laughter and snickering echoed through the room, and then everyone left. Everyone but me, that is. I stood, surrounded by the gore, and wondered how anyone could make jokes in front of two people they had just spent 40 minutes trying to revive. Maybe that's why this job is getting more and more difficult to tolerate for me. I have still held onto my emotions, while the professionals around me have abandoned them. I watch as the doctor, clad in blood-soaked scrubs, leaves the room, preparing to tell three people that their lives have changed irrevocably. He doesn't seem upset, or even stressed. He seems resigned, as though this is just an unpleasant chore. Kind of like taking out the trash.

And that is a typical day at work for me.

The Walk of the Dead

I punch out, limp to the garage on swollen feet, and try to remember where I parked my car. A group of construction workers are standing around, measuring a parking space for blasting. Funny how everyone's raises have been frozen but there is still an extraordinary amount of remodeling being done on every section of the hospital. I wonder if our CEO received his raise, and if he feels guilty about it. Probably not – more than likely thinks he deserves it, the greedy bastard.

I start the car, and immediately the stereo kicks into gear and begins blaring music at an alarming volume-music I really like, just not at this volume at 730 in the morning. It's a German metal group, and its brashness helps steady me for the night ahead when I'm driving in for a shift. But right now, I'm drained and not equipped to deal with it. Instead, I press the AM button and the smooth tones of the female newscaster fills my ears. War, death, politics – not exactly food for the soul, but I try to be informed about the world around me. It can get difficult, especially with everything I deal with at my job.

I pull out of the garage and onto the street, searching for my pack of cigarettes. I find them stuffed into the drink carrier and light one up, sucking in the smoke as deeply as I can. This is a habit that I hide from my co-workers because I don't want to hear a lecture every time I light up. I can comfortably refrain from smoking during my shift, and smoking on hospital premises has recently been banned. The hardcore smokers have found some places on the property to hide from security, but why risk it?

As I work my way through the morning traffic, the pictures start to float through my brain. The two people I had spent so much time and effort on were dead, and I just couldn't get over it. They had been in a terrible car accident, and the vehicle had ended up wrapped around a utility pole. The man and woman in the car were both in the front seat, and neither one of them had thought to secure their safety belts. The woman was the passenger, and was projected headfirst through the windshield. The man was driving, and most of the steering wheel had been imbedded into his chest. The EMTs had been talking in the hallway, and said that they had never seen carnage like that.

One of the firefighters on the scene performing extrication actually had to stop using the Jaws of Life in order to throw up on the side of the road.

Once they got to the ER, they were toast. It was like wading through a slaughterhouse when I walked into the trauma room where they had been laid out, head to head. They were oozing blood everywhere, and the male driver had been eviscerated by the steering wheel. Severed intestines hung out of his abdominal cavity, and I knew when I saw them that both of these poor people were destined to die in that room. I was tempted to turn around and leave, but that would have been a dereliction of duty. So I did my job and stared at them all the while, feeling as though I was doing them a disservice by not letting them die in peace.

Stop thinking about it, I tell myself. You'll be home soon and a good rest is just what you need. I'm almost home now, and I don't remember most of the drive. Autopilot is sometimes a good thing. I pull into the parking lot of my apartment building, an old brick structure that once served as a clothing mill. I slam the car door and hoist my bag onto my shoulders, looking forward to crawling into bed. I walk slowly, hanging my head and not responding to anyone – after a shift, I usually feel like a zombie without brains to eat. I don't want to talk or listen; I just want to tune out.

I finally reach the door to my apartment, shutting it behind me and leaning against it. My two cats meow and rub up against my legs, but I don't pick them up. I look to make sure they have food and water, and then I go into the bedroom. Stripping my scrubs off, I go into the bathroom and shake two sleep tabs into my hand. Then I collapse into bed, grateful that I have the night off today and I have nothing more to do for the next 36 hours other than sleep and do a load of clothes.

PMH (personal medical history)

It would probably be a good thing to fill you in on a few details before I keep going.

I live alone and I have no children. I've been married twice and both men cheated, so after the second divorce I decided to take a break from men and begin therapy instead. So, I have a standing date once a week with Lawrence, a kindly older man who has begun to help me untangle my personal life one strand at a time. He soothes me and makes me feel that I am a worthwhile person, something that I really need in my life.

My "nuclear" family is fractured. Both my parents died years ago, leaving me with an inadequate older brother who rarely speaks to me. I'm not heartbroken about this; as a matter of fact, it's been a relief not having to deal with his judgement of me and my life. He has been married for many years to a woman that, I'm convinced, is a demon sent from Hell. He has six children and an overbearing pair of in-laws that run his life. I don't envy him having to deal with all of this, and I have no idea how he really feels about it. The only thing I'm sure of is that he has no respect for my occupation; he made that very clear when I started working in the medical field.

I have friends, but I also have little tolerance for human company at this point in my life. I get irritated and bored very easily, and this makes having a close friendship difficult. I also avoid alcohol at all costs, not because I have a problem with it but because it makes me physically ill. This is also a deterrent, for more reasons than one. Almost every social activity revolves around going to bars, and someone who is sober never has a good time surrounded by drunks. And I always get stuck with the designated driver job, a chore I hate. Noone likes the smell of vomit, and getting it out of car upholstery is no easy task.

I always feel as though I'm with people who have no idea what's going on around them – they are more concerned about their little lives than anything else and this just seems so petty to me. Who said what to whom, what they said back, who's sleeping with whom in the call room at 3 am – these are not things that interest me. I want to feel connected to something deeper and bigger than myself, and it's hard to do that when you're sunk in the muck of daily nonsense.

Awake and Alert

Oh, the noise. I pull the covers off my head and slam my hand down on the alarm clock, which is buzzing so loudly it actually feels like it's burrowing into my head. I must have forgotten to turn it off today when I went to sleep. The clock reads 6 pm, usually the time I have to drag myself into the shower. It's okay, I tell myself. I really need to do laundry and my friends have been bothering me to get out more. I think I agreed to meet them at a bar later, something I am now regretting but it's too late to cancel now.

I walk over to the bathroom and turn on the shower, testing for the perfect temperature. I unleash my long hair from the bun it's been in since I got home and feel it cascade down my shoulders. I step into the shower and stand under the stream, letting the heat penetrate the pores of my face and scalp. Then the pictures start, a never-ending cycle of horrifying images. The blood, body parts, frozen faces and deadened eyes – this is pure fodder for the most disgusting horror movie. Unfortunately, it's real life, the life I've chosen. I shake my head and spray water everywhere, trying to rid myself of the film loop my brain has chosen to torture me with but nothing seems to work. So I finish showering and towel off, letting the images bounce off each other and finally fade into nothing. This is a daily part of my life as well, reliving the day's work. Some people come home, pop open a beer, and complain to anyone who will listen about their fat bitchy boss and the amount of paperwork they have to finish. I come home and have blood, phlegm, and bone dust floating around in my head. Furthermore, even if there was someone here, chances are very good that s/he would have a difficult time listening to what my day was like. It's just too much for most people – even my friends don't want to hear about it, though they say they admire me. "I could never do what you do," is a common sentence I hear – flattering, to say the least, but hardly a statement I can believe. It's meant as a compliment, but those words make me nervous-it places a great amount of responsibility on me, and I'm not sure I'm worthy of such trust and admiration.

I comb my hair and leave it hanging, then pull on underwear and bra. I search through my closet, looking for something suitable to wear and coming up with a pair of ripped jeans and a black tee-shirt. I pull them on and find my combat boots, lacing them up. These are the kind of outfits I wear constantly, and I like them. It may not be feminine or fashionable, but I've never been interested in looking a certain way in order to impress anyone. It's hard enough being comfortable in my own skin.

Finding my keys and getting out the door with my dirty laundry eats up 30 minutes, and by the time I reach the washer and dryer downstairs it's after 7pm. There's only one person in the laundry room, a man who lives across from me. He nods, I nod, and that's the end of it. As far as I know, he lives alone and seems to have very little connection with the outside world, and that's why I like him so much. No pressure to make conversation, no knowing looks – just sharing space for a few minutes. It's a relief, however, when he leaves without a word and I have the room to myself. I put the clothes in and switch on the machine, making sure the cycle is on the right temperature. Then I leave, preparing for the noise of the bar.

ETOH

The bar is crowded and noisy, not a big surprise. I walk through the swarm, being careful not to bump into anyone. My two friends are here, sitting at a table and already deep into their second beers. Four shot glasses have been emptied, and I sigh as I realize they are probably drunk already. Thia looks up and sees me, waving maniacally and giggling hysterically. I walk over and sit down, and Hannah immediately launches herself off her chair into my lap. She gives me a tight hug and buries her face in my hair, sniffing loudly.

"Oh baby we thought you weren't ever going to show up. Mmmm, you smell good enough to eat. What took you so long? Were you trying to find the ugliest clothes in your closet?"

"Funny. No, I worked last night and I had to shower and throw in my laundry. You should get off me if you want to get laid tonight, sweetie. You don't want all of these fine men to think you're a dyke."

"I'd rather sleep with you, but you have this whole isolation thing going. OK, are you going to have a drink this time or claim you're allergic to alcohol again? Thia, order her a shot and a beer."

"Why bother?" Thia shifts back in her chair and gives me a searching look. "I'll have to drink it myself – what a waste. Why do you insist on being sober every minute of the day? It's boring and unattractive to boot."

I turn to face her, Hannah almost sliding onto the floor when I do. "I don't insist on being sober, I insist on not projectile vomiting. I don't lie about that. Don't you think I wish I could get blasted once in a while? It would help."

"Yes, it would. Maybe you could stand having someone in your bed."

"Do we have to talk about my lack of a sex life every time we go out? I'm so bored with this."

"So are we. We worry about you, and we want you to be happy. Look, there's some fresh meat worth checking out – want to get a closer perspective?" Thia gets up from her seat and tries to pull Hannah off me, but Hannah is not cooperating. She grabs hold of my shirt and sticks her tongue out at Thia. "Leave us alone. Besides, there's no one here worthy of this princess." She tries to push her head under my shirt, which attracts the attention of three men at the bar. They start giggling like schoolboys looking at their first Playboy, and I immediately blush. Together Thia and I put Hannah back in her chair, where she proceeds to down the rest of her beer. Thia grabs my hand and pulls me over toward the band, who are playing a hideous version of the Police's "Message in a Bottle". She points at a table, and I see a man sitting by himself nursing a glass of whiskey. Thin, blond hair, and quite young – he probably got carded when he came in here. I shake my head and whisper in her ear, "No blondes. You know the rules." Thia gives me a disgusted look, and we move on. There's a group of bikers over in the corner, all muscle and mouth – definitely not my type either. I have a strong dislike to being called anyone's "old lady". We come full circle and return to our table, where Hannah is delightedly eyeing three fresh shots. "Look, more liquor. And I didn't have to pay for it!" She points over to the bar where a large, muscled man with long black hair is sitting. He's wearing a black shirt with what is supposed to look like blood splattered across it, black jeans, and Doc Martens. His lip is pierced, and his arms are covered with tattoos.

"Well, Hannah, looks like just the dark horse you've been searching for. Did you go over and introduce yourself, or just stick your tongue in his ear?" I grin and poke her in the ribs, and she looks up at me with a pout.

"He didn't buy this for me. He told the bartender to tell you that you should loosen up and have a few of those. Guess he was listening to our conversation and got a good laugh." Hannah grabs a glass and holds it in front of my face. "It would be rude not to accept. Besides, he looks like the type of guy you shouldn't piss off. He didn't even come over to give me the shots – he's been in that same seat the whole time." I look over at him, and he doesn't seem to notice. He continues to stare at the wall of bottles in front of him, not acknowledging anyone in the room. Maybe we have more in common than I think.

There's a sound of glass smashing in the corner, and one of the bikers barrels around the bar and stops in front of the mystery man. "Hey, asshole! Didn't you flip me off when we were pulling into the parking lot?" The biker is obviously drunk and ready for a fight. He's holding a beer bottle over his head, waiting for any response. The man at the bar turns around slowly and eyes up the biker, unimpressed by the weapon he's holding. "Look, dude, you cut me off on the way in here, so yeah I flipped you off. I'm not in the mood to fight, so why don't you go on back over to your little buddies and leave this alone." He turns around to resume staring at the wall, but the biker is having none of it. With a loud grunt, he swings his arm down intending to hit the man over the head. With one swift movement, the man at the bar catches the bottle in mid-air, comes face to face with the biker, and then sweeps both feet out from under him, the biker goes down hard, landing on his ass and back. The man looks down at him, shaking his head in disgust. "I told you to leave it alone. Now I have to go find someplace more quiet." He reaches in his pocket and pulls out a few bills, which he places carefully on the bar next to his empty mug. "Make sure that girl has a good time, will ya?" he says to the bartender and nods in my direction. "It looks like she's had a bad day." He looks me over, grins, and heads for the exit. Just my luck – a guy who likes to make a mess and leaves me to clean up. This is why I live alone.

Sleep Disturbance

After the debacle at the bar, I ended up driving Thia and Hannah home – I'm grateful that they live together and that noone threw up in my car. I come home to a dark apartment and slam the door behind me. I'm so happy that there is no noise to make the pounding in my head worse. I decide to leave the clothes in the washer – no one will want them, and I am too tired to care at this point. Despite sleeping for most of the day, I feel drained and empty. The only thing I want to do is crawl into my bed and turn the TV to some mindless nonsense. After some searching, I find my favorite nightgown and pull it on. Again, definitely not high fashion but very comfortable. I fold the covers of the bed down and turn on the small TV. It flashes and hums, finally lighting up the room. Perfect! A Family Guy marathon. I tuck myself into the sheets and close my eyes, preparing for the inevitable onslaught of images to cloud my mind. I have a hard time sleeping, for more than one reason. My brain just will not shut up, and everything that bothers me comes to the surface. Today it's the bodies in the trauma room – the blood, the body parts, the uncaring attitude of my co-workers. All of these things swirl around in my head, forming a funnel cloud of rage and sadness. I turn over and shift my body on the mattress, resigning myself to the fact that getting any sleep is going to be impossible. I sit up and grab the remote. It's going to be a long night.

The Board

I stand in front of it, not daring to touch it – the Board. The Board is a huge white dry-erase blackboard that has every area of the hospital represented by numbers and letters. Next to each area is a count of the number of work units for the shift. Each task has a value, and those are added up to represent the amount of work on any floor. I don't think there is any place in the whole department that is more negatively charged than the Board. It's here that everyone is assigned their work, and then the arguments ensue. The whining, the crying, the fighting – it reminds me of an overgrown preschool class where every student has missed their afternoon nap. I consider myself above all of this strife – I am a medical professional, after all. However, sometimes even I participate in the arguing just to join in the fun. Tonight I have no energy for it, and just sit down in front to await my assignment much the same way a convicted murderer awaits the electric chair.

Jerry walks down the hall and nods to me, carrying a cell phone. Jerry is the charge therapist for this shift, which means he is responsible for the assignments. He looks over the Board and then ducks into the computer room to print up a list of the patients we'll be caring for tonight. A few more people wander into the hallway and say hello, staring daggers at the Board as they walk by. I look over the numbers and they seem very high this evening – most of the people in the ICUs must be on ventilators. I take the clipboard that holds the list of therapists that will be working and count how many of us will be here – nine. Not too bad, although it never seems to be enough. Then I look at the bottom of the sheet and see two names written in the sick call column. Shit, that only leaves seven of us to cover 5 ICUs and all of the floors. Now I see why everyone appears to be too quiet. This is a common occurrence in the department and I'm not surprised, but it's not going to make the shift any easier to tolerate.

Staffing is one of the big problems not only in this department, but everywhere in the hospital. The only people we have too many of are the medical students – residents and interns who have no clue what's going on around them because they're too busy reading the latest journal articles. Nurses, respiratory therapists, surgical techs, all of us are overworked to the point where we just cannot take anymore. And to top it off, we have the responsibility of caring for human lives. We're not shuffling paperwork or selling computers or stocking shelves; we have the lives of thousands of people in our hands. Our actions can make or break the health and safety of our patients, and it's a daunting task. Understaffing makes this responsibility ten times more difficult to carry out, and the management never seems to understand this. Of course, the only thing they understand is the possibility of losing their budgets – a constant threat since the economy crashed and burned.

I see Carrie down the hall and walk over to where she's standing. Her huge pregnant belly is silhouetted against the wall, and I put my hand on it and grin up at her. Carrie is two days past her due date, and it's beginning to weigh on her. She grins back at me with heavily shadowed eyes and moves my hand to the other side of her stomach.

"He's over here today. And boy is he hungry!"

"Did you eat dinner yet?" I ask her.

"No," she says, moving aside to let someone pass through. "I had two transports in the last four hours and I had no time."

"Well, let's go get you a snack then. You shouldn't go this long without any food. You at least grabbed something to drink, right?"

Carrie pouted and shook her head. "I know I'm going to hear a lecture, but what was I supposed to do? Tell the nurse we had to postpone taking the patient to the OR because I was thirsty?"

"Yes. Travels get postponed and cancelled for the most asinine reasons and noone else seems to care. Why shouldn't you be allowed to get a drink for two minutes?"

"Oh, forget it," Carrie says and waves her hand in a dismissive gesture. "You know how it is. We're the bastard children of the hospital. They don't want to see us unless there's a problem, and then we can't get there fast enough. If I had asked for them to wait, I would have gotten a bad girl email."

"Fuck them. You're pregnant, for God's sake. You could go into labor at any moment – you shouldn't even be doing any transports. Whose bright idea was that?"

"Jerry's. He was supposed to take all of my travels, but he decided it would be a better idea to go get coffee at the shop down the street. I don't think he's done any work for the last 6 hours, the little shit."

"That's it. I'm going to talk to him about this." I turn to walk away but Carrie puts her hand on my arm to stop me. "Please don't," she says while looking around the corner. "You're going to get yourself in trouble for nothing. He doesn't care and he never will."

I pull away as gently as I can and look into her face. "I'm going to make him care, and if I get in trouble so what? It's not as if that's never happened before. He should get up off his fat ass and do some work like the rest of us." I strode down the hall to the computer room where Jerry is busy studying the sheets he's just printed out. I stand in front of him and wait for him to acknowledge my presence.

"Well, what is it? I'm about to make up the assignment. Do you have a special request?" He smirks at me, and I feel my face flush as anger floods my bloodstream.

"Where do you get off making Carrie take two transports? You're supposed to help during the shift if anyone needs anything. What, were you too busy buying coffee for that new nurse up on 7 so you can get into her pants later?" I see him stiffen in his chair, and I grin brightly at him. Jerry is not only lazy but very easily pissed off, and I can see I've gotten the response I was looking for.

"If she needed help, all she had to do was call." He gets up and shakes the handheld phone in my face. "You just punched in and you're already causing trouble. Don't you know that management is looking to lay off some workers? Keep this shit up, and I'll make sure you're the first name on the list."

I keep grinning and step closer to him, pushing my face into his. "Do I need to call the labor board and tell them that you are allowing a pregnant worker to go without a break? Or maybe your buddies down in Human Resources would be more interested. Where is that number?" I start to walk away and Jerry stands up to block my path. He's still angry but he knows I don't make empty threats, and now he's going to have to deal with me.

"Geez, are you her mother? Can't she speak up for herself?"

"You knew she had too much work and you let her do it anyway. Stop being lazy and help out, or those phone numbers will get utilized. Got it?" I can see the gears moving in Jerry's head, and he moves out of my way. "Fine. I'll make sure she has help. But you won't be the one assisting her. Just for that little outburst, you get to take the neuro unit all by yourself. Have fun," he giggles, and then he turns back to me. "By the way, that nurse up on 7 is only interested in females. Why don't you have a shot at her? Maybe you'll have better luck getting laid if you bat for the other team." I feel my hands clench into fists as I watch him take a marker and write my name next to the neuro assignment. I feel a hand on my shoulder and turn around to see Kate standing behind me.

"Just can't keep your mouth shut, can you? Now look at what you have to put up with tonight – I know the neuro unit is your least favorite thing to do." She's right, and I have the urge to fake sick so I can go home. The neuro unit is the most depressing place in the whole building as far as I'm concerned. Anyone with a brain issue goes there – trauma from a car accident, brain bleed, vegetative state, they all end up there. Rows and rows of rotting human flesh, just waiting for the day when their heart finally gives up the fight. Most of these patients are non-verbal and cannot even feed themselves, and there is always at least one crying family member in the hallway who wants to be told that everything is going to be normal again one day. It's the epitome of sadness and sorrow, and I have a hard time dealing with it. It reminds me of the way my mother acted when my dad was ill – she never even considered the possibility that he would die, and when he did she was totally unprepared for it.

I go into the computer room and pick up my sheets. One, two, three . . . there are twelve people on ventilators, and three more that need assistance with coughing and spitting up. This is not going to be pretty. I sigh and pick up the phone to call the unit.

"Neuro unit, can I help you?" A terse voice spits. "Can I speak to the respiratory therapist on duty, please?" "Hold," the voice states and then dead silence. At least I don't have to listen to muzak – that stuff makes me want to put a gun in my mouth.

"Hello, this is Lenny." Oh, great. Another slacker with an attitude – I'll have to spend half of my shift cleaning up his mess and placating the nurses on duty. Oh my, I think I might be coming down with H1N1 – please?

Report

My day in the neuro unit is finally over. I get down to the department just in time to see everyone on the day shift gathered around the Board, looking at what they're going to be doing today and getting anxious just thinking about it. The night shift was very busy – one car accident with three people, two stabbings, three shootings, and five alcohol withdrawals. They all required assistance breathing, and after some scrambling a bed was found for each of them. All of my co-workers and myself stayed at top speed all night, and now all we want to do is drive home without falling asleep at the wheel and fall into bed. But we can't yet – report is about to begin. This is the passing of the torch from one shift to the next, and it's a very important part of our work. Each patient we work with has a particular story, and we have to know at least most of it as intimately as we know our own. This is also the time to explain if there have been any problems, physically or emotionally. Some patients spit, bite, and try to hit. Other patients think you are their long-lost daughter. I have been slapped, hit, kicked, sworn at, bitten, shoved, and told to fuck off in the course of my career. It would have been helpful to know about these patients' proclivity toward violence, and so now I make sure to tell the next person if they will be having any issues.

"Who's taking the neuro unit?" I call out. A tall, thin man with a shiny bald head appears and gives me the finger, and I can't help but grin.

"Numb nuts. How the hell are ya?" I reach out and rub his head. "A little too much polish on there, big boy. Didn't I tell you to stop using the same shit you use on your bowling ball?"

"Ha ha ha. You know, shitbird, you really ought to have someone follow you everywhere you go and announce your presence before you arrive. It would be helpful for those of us who don't want to put with your crap. "

Jordan is one of the people I work with that I like and respect. He's a no-nonsense man, and tells it like it is whether you want to hear it or not. He's also very intelligent, and knows exactly what needs to be done and how to do it. Giving him report will be a breeze, and as we sit down at the table I breathe a sigh of relief. I will be able to punch out on time for once – and after the night I've had, getting out of here is a priority. I tell each patients' story as completely as I can, referring to my notes when I don't remember details. Jordan sits across from me, writing quickly and occasionally asking a question. Fifteen minutes later, we are all done and I grab my bag to head for the time clock. I start to head down the hall until I hear raised voices from the direction I just came from. Do I turn around and see what the problem is? Why not?

As I walk back the voices become louder and louder until I get to the doorway of the report room. Nancy is standing up, hands on her hips, shouting at none other than the man I had tangled with earlier – Jerry. He is also standing and shouting back.

"Why the hell would I want to take a floor assignment? It says right here on the rotation that I am the medical ICU therapist for the entire week. I've been there for three days already, and I know all of the patients. Why am I being moved?"

"Because I have to put the students in there and there aren't enough work units for you to share."

"Bullshit! There's plenty of work to go around in there. You just wanted to mess with me. I'm not going to put up with this – I'm walking down the hall to Todd's office." Nancy pushes past Jerry and the rest of the therapists in the room. She sees me standing at the doorway and pauses, then continues walking toward the manager's office. Jerry strides out of the room after Nancy, and the argument escalates into screaming and cursing. A door at the end of the hall flies open and Todd, the manager, walks out.

"OK, people, tell me what's happening out here. Perhaps a session of conflict resolution would be helpful to both of you. Why don't you come into the office and we'll all discuss it. OK?" Nancy and Jerry look at him and nod, and all three of them disappear into the open doorway. I stare, flabbergasted, as everyone else just goes back to report as though nothing happened. Jordan claps me on the shoulder. "Why so surprised, shitbird? You should know better than anyone what goes on around here on a daily basis. Go home and get some sleep – I have to give you report when you come in tonight." He points at me and then heads toward the elevator.

He's right, of course. This does happen every day, and yet I'm still shocked to witness it.

Guess I'm just too much of an optimist.

Anesthesia STAT

"Hey there. Are you covering us tonight?" A young, pretty nurse with long brown hair swept back into a ponytail hangs through the doorway where I'm charting. I'm not that familiar with this person but I have a sinking feeling that I'm going to have to get up immediately and abandon the flowcharts I've been trying to fill out for most of the shift.

"Yes, I am. Can I help you with something?"

"Well, my lady in 18 doesn't seem to be doing that well. I know that you checked on her earlier, but do you think you could go back in and see her? Her oxygen sats have been dropping into the 80s even with the mask."

I get up and smooth out my scrub top, logging off the computer after saving my progress. I already know which patient she's talking about, and it doesn't surprise me in the least to hear that she's not doing well. She is 85 years old and she was admitted here with a bout of pneumonia. To make matters worse, she also has dementia and a plethora of related medical problems, which makes her difficult to manage. She is what we call in the medical profession a "train wreck". Fixing all of her problems would be impossible; we just bounce from crisis to crisis and keep her alive the best way we know how.

I follow the nurse down the hall to Room 18 and peer inside. My patient, obese and white-haired, lays lifeless in her bed. The BIPAP machine is humming, the mask is on her face, and she appears to be making an effort to breathe. Then I look up at the monitor and see that her O2 sat is 79%; this isn't looking good.

"What's her code status?" I look out of the doorway and see the nurse looking it up in the chart.

"She's full. There was a family meeting today and her children were fighting about what to do about it. Most of them want her to just be comfortable, but her eldest daughter is a doctor and insisted that we do everything."

"Well, you better find her number and wake her ass up. She's about to get exactly what she wants because this woman needs to be intubated and moved into the ICU. Call the resident first and get him over here now." The nurse looks both confused and scared, like a deer caught in the headlights of a tractor trailer. I move over to her desk and look into her face. "Do what I said, and do it now. Otherwise this woman is going to die right here in this room." My words seem to have the right effect; she picks up the phone to page the resident and I move into action. I find the code cart and move it into the room, setting up equipment as I go. The resident appears, a man in a white lab coat who looks like he just graduated high school. He is tired, rumpled, and confused. "What's going on?" he says as he leans over the bed. He tries to get a response out of the patient but she has nothing to say. He tries to pinch her and calls her name loudly but she continues to lie there, shaking like a leaf and struggling to breathe. I pull off the BIPAP mask that has been strapped to her face and replace it with a bag mask, pumping pure oxygen into her lungs by squeezing the reservoir.

The resident scratches his head and asks,"When was the last time you got her to respond?" I look over at him and suppress the urge to slap him across the face. "I'm not the nurse. She's out at the desk looking up phone numbers. I don't think you understand – she needs to be tubed ASAP." He looks at me with a mixture of arrogance and annoyance. "I think we should at least get some blood work first. No point in jumping the gun here. Besides, look how old she is. She's probably a no-code anyway." He turns to leave and I grab his arm with one hand while still bagging with the other. "I already asked and she is a full code. I know you haven't worked in an actual hospital before so let me give you a tip. It's now 4 am – the time when the bed manager starts giving away whatever ICU beds are left, and there are never that many of them. I will bet my annual salary that this woman will end up being put on a ventilator sooner rather than later, and she's going to need a bed. Call anesthesia stat now, and she can have the last bed next door. If you wait, someone is going to ask why. Do you want to face that, or just listen to me? " He looks at me and I wait, knowing that I'm right and hoping he believes me. His face softens as he thinks about what I've said, and then he walks out. "Call anesthesia stat, and the senior resident."

More than twenty people crowd the room, including my co-worker Tom who has been playing an online game. "'What do you need?" he says while breaking open the seal on the code box. "Set up an 8 with a MAC 3 blade, and please make sure the suction is operating." He moves quickly to fill my request, and then the room explodes into chaos. There are people yelling for drugs, doctors reading the chart aloud, nurses moving IV poles out of the way, and I feel like the very center of a hurricane. I'm surrounded by mess and flurry, and yet I am still and calm. I continue pumping air through the bag, watching with detachment and amusement as all these people who claim to be professionals work themselves into full-blown panic. This is how it always happens, and it surprises me every time.

Tom moves into the gap next to me and joins me in my pocket of calm; he seems even more amused than I am. He puts his hand on the bag and looks at me and I shake my head. I don't need a break; at moments like these I could go forever. There's adrenaline pumping through me like fire in my veins, and it's being fueled by the frustration I feel with all of the other people in the room who are doing nothing to save this poor woman's life. I was tired and nauseous before this happened, but that has vanished. I have never done any hard drugs, but this is definitely what an addict must feel right after shooting up-no pain, no fatigue, nothing but energy. It's a high that I look forward to, because I finally feel at that moment that I'm doing something with a purpose.

The breathing tube goes in smoothly and the doctor calls for an x-ray to check the placement. I continue pumping the bag, watching to make sure the chest rises and falls. Tom leaves the room to find a ventilator and the rest of the crowd follows him. I'm left alone with the patient, who is now lying in the bed quietly. Her color is better and she has stopped sweating; she looks peaceful, and as I watch her face I wonder if any thoughts are going through her head. It's difficult to tell, considering the fact that her body was flooded with sedatives right before the tube was placed in her throat. I'm just grateful to see that she is not struggling any longer; I'm also getting tired of squeezing the bag and my hand is beginning to cramp up.

Suddenly there is a high-pitched noise, and I look up at the monitor to see what the problem is. The patient's heart rate has ceased, and the noise is the heart alarm. One second goes by that is filled with complete silence, and I look down at the woman to see the same peaceful expression that was there before. My stomach thumps and sinks, and I realize that death is going to visit this room shortly. What happens next is a blur-

everyone comes back into the room, the defibrillator is pushed in, there is shouting and running. More drugs are measured into syringes and pushed into the IV line, but the heart monitor stubbornly refuses to change from its flat pattern. A burly male aide dressed in white appears and begins to pound on the woman's chest over and over; I change the rhythm of my squeezes to match his compressions. Tom reappears wheeling a machine, sees what is going on, and abandons the equipment in the hallway.

"You've been bagging for over an hour. Give it to me and go get a drink-you're dripping sweat." I shake my head but he has already foreseen this and grabs the bag from my hand. "I'm not asking, I'm telling. Get in the hallway. You've done enough for one shift." He begins squeezing just as I had been doing, and I walk into the hall. I get back pats and words of praise from the nurses and doctors standing there, but I don't seem to really hear them. I go find a chair and sit down, massaging my hand which is now sore. A few minutes later, I see people leaving the room I was in with slow steps. A group of doctors are sharing the chart amongst themselves and one of them is telling a dirty joke which is received with loud laughter. There is only one person I see who shows any feeling for the poor woman in the bed who has just died; Tom walks out with his head down and collapses into the chair next to me.

"Well, just another day in the slaughterhouse I guess. You OK?" Tom leans over me and looks into my face. "Yeah, I'm fine. I just never seem to be able to shake my feelings when something like this happens. I didn't even know this lady, and I feel so sad for her. You know?"

"Don't worry. Keep doing this for a few more years and you'll eventually end up like them." He points to the group of doctors with the chart, who are still laughing and telling jokes. "They don't ever seem to give a rat's ass who dies. Why should you?" He gives me a crooked smile and gets up. "Back to the grindstone. Want some coffee?" I nod my head and he puts his hand on my arm. "I know you're upset but don't let yourself get depressed. You did a good job in there. It's not your fault she died." He walks away to the pantry and I watch, envious that I'm surrounded by people who have all their emotions in check.

Sherlock Holmes

Just in case you didn't know, medicine is not an exact science. The scrubs and lab coats that medical workers wear is a façade to gain your confidence; they should really be wearing a costume reminiscent of Sherlock Holmes. Why? Because that would be more honest – everyone in the hospital is an apprentice detective. All of them are there to gather clues; symptoms, medical history, lab tests. These bits of data are all clues that are put together to create a picture, even if it's incomplete. Once the picture emerges, it's brought to the head detective – the doctor. An experienced doctor will look not just at the picture but also the gaps in its structure; then a decent diagnosis can be achieved. A doctor just out of school or one that is a poor detective will take the picture at face value and make choices based on the incomplete vision that has been placed in front of him/her. This leads to bad decisions, sometimes even death. But it's the way the system has worked for centuries, and for the most part it is trusted implicitly.

This is not the way the medical system is portrayed to the rest of the world; it looks very complicated from the outside. It also looks perfect, more perfect than the people who enter it. Anyone with a medical degree is seen as competent, intelligent, and caring. But, every person is a human being, no matter how many letters come after their name. They have the same flaws, the same problems, and the same range of intelligence. They lose their temper and make terrible mistakes just like everyone else – the difference is, the human errors made in the hospital can cost someone their life.

I am a cog in the hospital machine, and my title is respiratory therapist. Not a well-known occupation, but a very important one. I am responsible for any patient with any kind of lung disorder, and the list of lung diseases is quite long. I also care for patients who need to utilize mechanical ventilation, or "life support" as it's called in popular culture. I make sure they are getting the right amount of air and oxygen, I suction phlegm out of their lungs when they can't cough, and sometimes I turn off the machine when their families have decided their family member needs some peace in their final moments.

I love my job, but there are moments when I want to rip every hair out of my head because I just can't do everything myself. I can't write the orders for medication that I know the patient needs to calm down, I can't wipe someone's backside when they've been sitting in their own shit for hours, I can't loosen the restraints binding their wrists. Those jobs belong to other people, and for the most part no one seems to have one brain cell between themselves that they can share. Not only that, but there are lots of hospital workers who care more about their coffee break than the needs of the patients. Doctors are commonly characterized as greedy, but don't be fooled. Greed runs rampant in every hospital – it is a business, after all, and the goal of business is to make as many fat wallets as possible. If doctors make money, so does everyone else around them.

So the next time you're tempted to trust someone in a lab coat, think about that. You just might be tempted to hit the Internet for some impromptu Googling.

The Hierarchy

Just like every good organization, there is a system of categorizing employees in the hospital. It is set up to work as a well-oiled machine, but ends up looking and acting like a soggy seven layer dip. The top layer is, of course, the upper management – these people are rarely seen in person but figure prominently in emails and cyberspace. They rarely mix with anyone else in the building unless it occurs in a conference room, and they have very little knowledge of the day-to-day operations. Nonetheless, these people are the ones who make the most money and are responsible for the hospital's outer image.

The second layer consists of middle management – nurse managers, educators, and other department bosses. These are people that usually have some form of practical experience and in theory should be sympathetic to the workers. Unfortunately, there seems to be no human emotion detectible, and I secretly believe that anyone accepting one of these jobs has to go through a brain scan to remove all feelings from their system. These people are not that effective at running anything, much less a bunch of pissed-off and tired workers. They try to avoid human contact, and instead prefer to issue orders via their email inbox. A personal meeting with one of these managers means that you have caused enough trouble to make waves – and waves need to be stopped as soon as possible.

The third and fourth layers contain the medical workers – and this is where the dip gets really messy. Doctors are, of course, on the top, followed by nurses. These two groups usually work together and often at odds with the rest of us – the fourth layer. We are the more specialized workers, the ones who deal with one topic of a patient's care. We take the orders that are written by the doctors and communicated to us by the nurses, and we turn it into reality. Breathing treatments, x-rays, blood work – whatever is needed, we perform it. Nurses also carry out orders, but they seem to feel as though they are an extension of the doctors and try their best to make sure the rest of us know they are in charge. There is a constant push and pull between these layers, as we are all highly trained and educated. Everyone thinks their idea is the right one, and this is the cause of a lot of the waves the middle management ends up having to quell.

The last three layers of the dip are very important but ignored by most of the people in the hospital. The invisible workers – housekeeping, food service, engineering, security – are responsible for keeping the building clean and safe. They cook and deliver the food that feeds the patients, they guard every entrance and exit, they clean hallways and rooms. If these people didn't exist, there would be utter chaos. But, since they are often not medically educated, they are looked down upon and dismissed. I always go out of my way to be polite and gracious to these workers, and say thank you every time I see them.

The dip is laid out, and the patient is the chip that gets plunged into the container. Anyone who's been at a party knows how the dip looks at the end of the party – multicolored mush with puddles of sour cream in the middle. It's the luck of the draw when it comes to which layer you get more of, unless you are one of the smart ones who knows when and where to place your chip.

First Date

I wake up to the sound of my phone vibrating – who the hell wants to talk to me at 3 in the afternoon? Obviously noone who knows me or my schedule – none of my friends would even dare to leave a text at this time of the day. I roll over slowly and pick up my phone, cursing under my breath as I do so. I look at the screen and it informs me that I have a voice message from an unknown number. I dial up and listen as a deep male voice talks into the phone, a voice I don't recognize. He says his name is Sid, and that Hannah gave him my number. That bitch! This is the guy from the bar, the dark horse who left the biker broken on the floor before he left. Why, oh why, do I have to deal with this?

I get up out of bed and pull on some clothes, then I go into the kitchen and pour myself some iced coffee from a pitcher in the fridge. Never forget that caffeine is your best friend when you work off-shifts. I add cream and sugar, then take the glass with me into the living room. I sit down and stare at the phone, wondering if I should call this person back or just ignore the message. I haven't had a date in months, and I didn't miss it. Dressing up in something you think is appropriate, driving to the meeting point, sitting at a table and nodding as the man in question tells you why you should sleep with him – it seemed very pointless to me. I met both of my husbands this way, and look at what happened. I have no need for sex, as Thia recently introduced me to the x-rated shop down the street from her apartment. I can pick up anything there, and it is always a crowded place. I've gotten so attached to my vibrator that I was thinking of throwing a commitment ceremony for the two of us. Now I'm faced with the actual possibility of sex with a man, and it frightens me a little. After draining the contents of my glass, I pick up the phone and dial.

"Hello, how can I help you?" Larry doesn't have a receptionist and always insists on answering his phone, a habit I find quaint and comforting.

"Larry, it's me. Do you have a minute for a question?"

"Never too busy for you , my dear. Just let me clear up a little problem here – put you on hold?"

"Sure," I say, and wait while he gets rid of whatever client is bending his ear. He is a popular therapist, and I never see him idle. I guess there are a lot of people in need of his assistance, just like me.

The phone clicks and I hear Larry's voice. "OK, what's your question? Is this something urgent? You know we have our date scheduled for tomorrow." He calls every appointment a "date", an inside joke because he knows about my lack of a social life.

"Yeah, it's not urgent, but I need to do something about it today. I've been asked out and I'm not sure if I should go"

"Is this the man you told me about last time? The guy in the bar?"

"Yep, the very one."

"Well, do you feel safe with this man?" Larry also knows about my lack of trust when it comes to anyone I'm romantically interested in.

"Yes, relatively. I think it's safe to say he can take care of himself. And I didn't get any bad feelings when I met him."

"Then why the confusion? Go out and have a good time for once. You know it's unhealthy to avoid relationships." I could almost hear him waggling his finger at the receiver.

"Yes, but what if I don't feel the need for one? I'm happy with my life the way it is."

Larry clucks his tongue and emits a sigh. "If you were that happy, you wouldn't be seeing me, now would you? This is something we've been working on for months, and now you have a candidate to practice on. Take a chance – it might work out. At the very least, you'll get a nice meal you won't have to pay for."

"All right, all right. But if I have a terrible time I'm getting my next session free. Deal?"

"Deal. You can tell me all about it tomorrow. Have a great time, and use a condom."

"Not funny. Bye."

I hung up and dialed the unknown number. Sid answered after the fourth ring. "It's your dime, so talk it up," he said.

"Hi, you called me and left a message? My friend Hannah gave you my number?"

"Oh, yeah. The chick in the bar – the only one with Doc Martens on. How are you? I didn't wake you, did I? Your friend told me you work the graveyard shift."

"Yeah I do, and as a matter of fact you did wake me. But you can make it up to me by buying me dinner tonight."

"Tonight, huh? You don't waste time, do you?"

"Why bother? Life is short and time is fleeting. So are you up for it?" I held my breath and waited for his answer.

"Sure, why not? I need a break from working out this riff anyway. You want me to pick you up, or would you rather meet me somewhere?"

I named a restaurant that was down the street from my apartment, a little hole in the wall with a fabulous menu and cheap prices. "Meet you there at 5?"

"Yep. I'll see you there." He hung up, and I put the phone down on the table. I stroked the cat that had curled up in my lap while I was talking and closed my eyes. Will this be fun, or yet another colossal waste of time? I get up from the couch to turn on the shower.

Vital Signs

As I drive up to the restaurant, I look at myself in the rearview mirror. Minimal makeup? Check. Nondescript clothing? Check. Hannah and Thia would freak out if they saw me, but I really don't care. I just want to get this over with and get my free session with Larry. I walk up to the heavy wooden door and open it, peering inside. The crumbling brick walls hold posters of blues bands, and the tables are mostly empty. There's no hostess, and I choose a deep booth at the back of the room. I ease into the seat and relax into the faux leather seat, breathing deeply as I do. A grumpy waitress peels herself off of a bar stool and sidles over, barely lifting her feet off the floor.

"What can I get for you?" She takes a pen out of her pocket and holds it poised over a ripped and dirty pad.

"Just a diet soda for now. I'm waiting for someone."

"Oh, you mean the freak over at the bar? Good luck with that piece of meat." She shuffles back to the bar and taps on the back of someone in the shadows. Sid gets up and strides to the booth, sliding into the opposite side.

"Thought you weren't going to show. I've been waiting for a half hour." He grins, and I noticed how perfect his teeth seem. His hair, coal-black, hangs past his shoulders in damp tendrils. His deep brown eyes have a mischievous twinkle in them, and his pierced lips are crimson and full. Easy, girl, easy.

"I believe the time we agreed on was 5 pm. It's not my fault if you can't tell time." The waitress slams the drinks down onto the table and I take a deep gulp from mine.

Sid picks up his beer and brings it to his lips. "Nervous, huh? Your friend told me you haven't had a date in quite some time. Don't worry, I'll go easy on you today." Damn, Hannah, I think I may have to disembowel you.

"I don't need anyone to go easy, Sid. I also don't need a smartass in my life – I have enough of those already. Know what? This was a mistake. I'll walk myself out." I move to the end of the booth to get up and Sid grabs my arm. Little jolts of electricity travel up my shoulder and into my face.

"Hey, don't leave. Please. I'm sorry – I'm not used to making idle chitchat and I'm rusty. Give me another chance?" He flashes those beautiful teeth again, and I sigh. I slowly remove his large, tattooed hand from my forearm and sit back down.

"OK, one more chance. I'm only here to make sure my friends don't put an ad in the personals on my behalf, but I don't see why I shouldn't have fun while I'm at it. Let's get something to eat and we'll see how it goes. Good for you?"

"Perfect. I'm beginning to like you already." Sid lifts his beer for another swig.

"Let's not get carried away. I'm not what you would call a personable human. And my friends are right, I haven't had a date in some time simply because I'm unable to tolerate bullshit. You may be in for a very bumpy ride."

"What luck – that's my favorite kind." Sid raises his eyebrow and gives me a smile. Oh boy, what did I get myself into?

Dinner is strange, bizarre, and very enjoyable. Sid tells me he is a musician, and specializes in black metal. He plays the bass, the drums, and sings – if growling can be considered singing. As he talks about his latest project, he takes on a very different vibe from the one he's presented to me before. He becomes playful, excited, vibrant – and unfortunately this only makes him more attractive. He taps out beats for me on the table with his fingers and hums some bars from his latest song, which annoys the hell out of the waitress who brings us our food.

I try not to talk about work, especially during the meal – most people I come into contact with don't appreciate hearing about what I sucked out of a patient's lung while they're trying to enjoy their gooey French onion soup. Sid, on the other hand, is just the opposite – he encourages me to tell my stories. He even seems to enjoy them – a fact that is not lost on me. It's very rare to find anyone who wants to hear about human suffering.

The date ends with a firm handshake in the parking lot – no one-night stands for me anymore. Sid waves goodbye and hops on his purple motorcycle. I get into my car and sit, wondering if I'll ever see him again.

Do We Need to Debrief?

Picture in your mind a large sitting room, complete with worn furniture, scrappy house plants, and dogeared magazines with photos of grinning celebrities. A radio is turned on for background noise; it's tuned to a 24-hour talk channel. It's a place for reflection and even relaxation.

Now picture me in the middle of this room, pacing a hole into the antique braided carpet.

I'm here for my weekly "date" with Larry, something that I usually look forward to. It's a chance to unload the weight of tension that builds up daily between my shoulder blades. It also carries zero guilt, which is how I feel when I talk to a relative or friend about my issues. Larry is someone very skilled that I pay to listen to me, and that makes all the difference in the world. But today I'm edgy, because I know the first and possibly only topic of today's conversation will be my date. And that is something I am not anxious to discuss.

Larry emerges from his office accompanied by a harried-looking woman who is holding a wad of tissues. Her eyes are puffy and red, and she avoids looking into my face. She shakes hands with Larry and stumbles out into the alcove, pulling her coat around her. I can only imagine what she and Larry were discussing, and I don't envy her psychic load.

"Well, well, well, look what the cat drug in," Larry exclaims, taking my hand in both of his and shaking it vigorously. "You look like you've seen a ghost. Let's go in and talk, shall we?" He relieves me of my coat and hangs it on a precariously balanced coat rack, then ushers me into the inner office. The office is dimly lit with one lamp and smells of cinnamon. There are two chairs and a couch, all upholstered with shabby chintz. A desk in the background is overrun with piles of paper and an opened laptop, and there are travel posters of different countries hanging on the paneled walls. I sit in one of the chairs, sinking into the cushion instantly. Larry seats himself in the opposite chair and opens his notepad. I shift in my chair and sigh, looking at the walls.

"So, not willing to talk today, huh? Probably because you don't want to admit that you lost our bet." Larry uncaps a pen and begins to write. "So, do I have to prod you or are you going to tell me what happened on your date?"

"Nothing, really. I just had dinner with the dude. He seems nice enough, but I don't think I'm ready to start dating anyone seriously. I have too many trust issues."

"Now that is one of the biggest pieces of bullshit I've ever heard. And I hear a lot of things that make me shake my head in wonder. Why won't you give this person a chance? Or are you too scared?" Larry shakes his pen at me, and I am shocked. Usually the vague psychobabble I offer up is enough to satisfy him; I guess this time I'm actually going to have to open up.

"OK, fine. Yes, I'm petrified. This guy is attractive, strange, and intelligent. I have a good chance of falling for this person, and I don't even want to think about what might happen if I do. Look at me – I have two failed marriages under my belt. I'm practically a recluse according to my friends, and my job is so stressful I need a therapist to deal with it. I am no prize for anyone."

"Noone is expecting you to be a prize. You just need to be yourself, and everything will come together." Larry leaned forward in his chair and tapped his pen on his forehead. "Remember how I always say that you don't need to have people in your life who aren't nice to you? There is a flipside to that statement – we all need nice people to lean on once in a while. People you don't pay." He snorted in laughter and made a note on the pad. "Believe me, I know where you're coming from. But I also know deep down inside, in places you don't talk about at parties, that you want someone to help you through all the shit you deal with. That person will be hard to locate, but hiding yourself away will ensure that you never find him."

I stood up and walked to the window seat. "I don't know, Larry. This guy I met – he's a musician, he's cute, he's smart, but . . . I can't see how dating him will help. The work I do, the things I see – it's enough to make a normal person go insane. I don't think it's fair to bring anyone into my personal hell."

"Why not let him make that decision for himself? He's an adult, isn't he? Maybe he's the man that can take it and not crumble. I know taking a chance is difficult, but I would hate to see you cement yourself into a lonely existence if you don't have to." Larry stood up and joined me at the window. "Now where's my check, you deadbeat? No welching." I reached in my pocket and handed the check to him while sticking out my tongue. He chuckled and took it. "I'll make you a deal. If you have a second date with this gentleman, I'll rip this up. OK?"

"Fine. Should I wait until he calls me or should I call him?"

"What am I, your mother? You figure it out. Now let's talk about the rest of your week."

Sick Time

There is some noise in the break room, a dark area of the department that is never used. I wander down the hallway and stop in the doorway. Sprawled out on the long table is Evan, a newcomer to the wonderful world of respiratory care. He opens his eyes, sees that it's me, and sighs with relief.

"I thought the jig was up. Thank God it's you." He sits up and takes a tissue out of his pocket to wipe his nose. "I've been in here trying to get a rest so I can finish the rest of the shift."

"Why, what's wrong with you?" I lean down and feel his forehead – hot and clammy, not good signs.

"I think it might be that stomach virus that's going around, but I can't afford to call out. I was puking my guts out for most of the day today but the attendance policy is so strict that I would have gotten written up if I had called out. So here I am." Evan pulls himself to a sitting position and hangs his head.

"Well, let me get you a glass of water at least." I turn to walk out but Evan puts a firm hand on my shoulder.

"I can't keep anything down. But thanks anyway. Could you… um…just not tell anyone you saw me in here? My beeper will wake me up if I'm needed."

"Sure." I walk over to the wall and flick off the light. Evan gives me a weak wave and lays back down on the table.

As I walk back down the hallway, I think about the extreme irony of this situation. We are hospital workers dealing with sick and injured patients, many of whom are at greater risk of infection than the general population. It would only make sense that, if a worker is sick, that s/he would not come to work. But the attendance policy usually prohibits more than one or two days of sick time a year. This includes any illness or injury, and a doctor's note is not considered a sufficient excuse. So workers fearing for their jobs come for their shifts no matter what kind of condition they're suffering from. This in turn leads to patients being exposed to all kinds of germs and viruses that could potentially kill them. If this doesn't make any sense, don't worry. You're not crazy – it doesn't make sense. But you have to remember that the people who make the rules aren't in the trenches – they have a very limited view from their offices on the top floor. And I can almost guarantee that they don't need to worry about sick time.

Bloody Hell

"Hey, did you hear what the overhead page just said? My pager didn't go off for it." Jordan pats me on the head and flicks my ear. I swat at him but he moves deftly away, laughing. I look down at my shirt and unclip one of the beepers that are hanging there. It may seem like an odd place to put them, but clipping them to my belt is not an option – they're so heavy, I may end up flashing a patient. A little cleavage is definitely preferable to a mooning.

"It's for the 14th floor ICU – the cardiac unit. Who's up there right now?" Jordan walks over to the board and scans. "Lenny – but I just saw him walk down the hall."

"Shit. Someone needs to go up there now – a new heart is tanking." I get up and grab my papers. Jordan blocks my way in the door. "Why does it have to be you, squirt? You aren't even assigned to cover that section." I push my way past him and yell over my shoulder. "It's not about who is covering what – it's about who is going to help the patient. And since Lenny doesn't seem to care, someone else needs to." Jordan follows me to the elevator, shaking his head in disbelief. I wave and grin as the doors close; he gives me the finger.

The doors open on the 14th floor; I rush past the surprised looks of visitors waiting for the elevator. I run down the hall and come to the double doors of the ICU; there are three people in the hall pacing. One woman, dressed in a torn tee shirt and dirty jeans, is crying in a corner with her hands over her face. These must be the relatives of the patient inside, and I can't afford to get caught up in the drama. I scan my badge on the electronic eye, making my face as blank as possible. The doors pop open and I rush in, avoiding the glances of the other people in the hall.

I see a crowd of people standing outside the #4 bed, and I push my way through. Inside the room is the patient, lying on his back. He is the color of an in-season plum, clearly not breathing. An intern is standing over the patient with a look of sheer panic on his pale face. I grab the lapels of his crisp lab coat and turn his body so that he is facing me.

"Who's the surgeon who operated on this patient today? Do you know what's going on?" I look up into his face and see no change in his expression. "Wake up, you moron – you need to start giving some orders so we can save this person." He seems to hear me but is still not moving. There is a commotion outside the door, and Janet appears –

the best cardiac nurse in the whole building. This is obviously her patient, and I am utterly grateful. At least now something will be done.

"OK, hotshot, get the bag out. Doctor, go make yourself useful and call Dr. Hillyer – he's going to want to know about this." Janet stares at the intern, who is still making no moments. She snaps her fingers in front of his face and he appears to wake up out of a dream, looking at her as though they've never met. "Doctor, did you hear me? You need to go call everyone in here and secure an OR. You need to page Dr. Hillyer and tell him his patient is shitting the bed. NOW!" The last syllable, yelled into his face, seems to give the intern the kick in the ass he needs. He takes out his cell phone and starts dialing numbers, walking out of the room as he does so. Janet looks at me and shrugs; I can only lift my eyebrows in response, as I have already attached the resuscitation bag to the wall oxygen and am pumping breaths into the patient. His color has already changed from plum to faded bruise, and he is beginning to make faint noises. I continue squeezing, and I watch as his oxygen saturation climbs slowly into the low 90s. Janet and another nurse are scurrying around the bed, adjusting IV medications. The intern returns carrying a plastic bag and the patient's chart.

"Dr. Hillyer was in the call room so he'll be right down. I called the OR and they said they are all full up at the moment." He is flushed and sweaty; Dr. Hillyer must have been taking out some frustration on this poor inexperienced soul.

"Did you tell the OR it's a cardiac emergency and that the patient just got out of surgery an hour ago? For Christ sake, who's running the asylum down there today?" Janet runs out of the room and slams headlong into Dr. Hillyer. He is a tall man, thin, but stands as though someone has just rammed an iron rod up his ass. He's wearing wrinkled scrubs and his glasses are askew on his face; he must have been catching up on some sleep when the intern paged him.

"What the fuck is going on in here? I just sent this guy to the PACU a few hours ago." He moves Janet out of the way and then storms into the room, almost knocking down the intern. "Why is he crashing like this? Have you even looked at his most recent labs?" He snatches the chart off the counter and flips to the middle. After a few seconds, he hands the chart to the intern and comes toward the bed. The patient is now awake with his eyes half-open, and Dr. Hillyer smiles at him to ease some of the tension. He motions for me to take the mask off for a few moments, and I oblige.

"Hey there, John. What's going on in here? I told you to behave when they put you in your room, and here you are making trouble." The patient tries to speak, but no sounds come out of his mouth. He smiles, and for a second I think everything's going to balance out. Dr. Hillyer turns away just in time to miss the patient's face collapse in pain; his eyes become wide, then roll back until I see only white. I place the mask back over his face as the monitor starts alarming; the heart rate and blood pressure are plummeting.

"Call anesthesia and prep me now. I'll have to crack him here." Dr. Hillyer looks at me and nods. "You've done an open heart before up here, right?" I nod and his face relaxes. "I know I can count on you and Janet to help me through this, OK?" He hurries out to the hallway and begins shouting orders to the crowd, who scatter to fulfill his needs. I am left alone in the room with the patient, and I look into his face for any sign of life – there is none, and I think about his relatives crying in the corridor. I hope we can save him, at least so that those poor people can see him one more time.

A plethora of staff crowd the room, all with a designated duty to perform. Within five minutes, the room looks like a mini OR, complete with a sterile table by the bed and a ventilator in the corner. The patient has been intubated, sedated, and prepped; Dr. Hillyer stands ready with a scalpel.

"OK people, ready? I need to crack his chest using the original incision and find out what's causing all this trouble. Those of you with weak stomachs should probably not be in here." Noone moves, and he begins. Scalpel, rib spreader – the organs are displayed in living color, and I hear someone gasp. This is not work usually done in a patient's room, and very few staff members outside of the OR ever see the inside of a patient in this manner. The heart is pumping and the lungs expand and retract; it's almost too real. Dr. Hillyer looks closely at the heart muscle he just repaired hours ago, and an expression of revelation appears on his face.

"I'm afraid John has a nasty case of cardiac tamponade. That would explain his vitals. Tim, come have a closer look – I didn't have you suit up for nothing." The intern I was dealing with earlier steps forward and moves toward the bed. He gets up behind Dr. Hillyer and takes a look into the opened cavity of the patient. For a moment he appears very interested; then his eyes roll back into his head and he passes out. Janet catches him with a disgusted look and passes him off to a burly male aide, who half-drags him into the hall.

"Well, I guess we can't count on him for the next surgery, huh? All right, let's drain the cavity and get this man up and running again." Dr. Hillyer looks at me and smiles. "You should have been a doctor, young lady. Nerves of solid steel. Thanks for being here." He turns his attention back to the patient, and I glow with the praise I've just been given. Compliments in this place are few and far between, and a compliment from a cardiac surgeon is almost unheard of.

Practice Makes Perfect

I take my coffee into the break room and slump into a chair, sighing as I do so. Dr. Hillyer successfully drained the cardiac cavity of the leaking blood and put his patient back together again. After he left the ICU eventually settled down, but it took a while and the stress of the crisis was evident on everyone's faces. Events such as these really make me wonder how many mistakes are committed in the OR.

Mistakes are a common topic of conversation in any hospital, and this one is no exception. I have heard horror stories that would rival any slasher flick – body parts set on fire by faulty lasers, body parts removed without consent, drunk and stoned surgeons. This is not unusual conversation around the dinner table in the cafeteria, but it's strictly forbidden outside the hospital. We, as a medical community, are expected to stick together through any kind of situation – even if it means we are covering up information from patients and family members. Legally, no detail of a patient's stay is to be repeated to anyone who is not caring for him/her, and there is to be no information sharing of any kind. However, there are ways around all of these stringent rules, and of course there is the fact that every hospital is a rampant rumor mill. The rumors are both personal and professional – as long as names are left out or changed, facts can be shared with everyone. And there are so many strange things that happen in a hospital at any time.

The emergency room is usually the place where the juiciest stories can be found. They range from violent acts to bizarre accidents. Patients suffering from gunshot wounds and stab wounds have been dumped from fast-moving vehicles onto the sidewalk outside the ER. Some patients have no identification and are classified as John/Jane Does for weeks until someone figures out who they are. And I don't think I need to go into the enormous list of things that have been stuck in a patient's orifice and need to be removed surgically. These are the stories that are passed from department to department and the stories become distorted each time one person repeats them. It's cruel and irresponsible, but I have to admit it also breaks the tension of an extremely stressful job. It's something to crack a smile over, and sometimes that overrules the restrictions.

Withdrawal Symptoms

One of the most colorful patients I have ever encountered I will call Jimbo Jones. Mr. Jones was admitted for an infection he received from shooting up heroin. There was an enormous hole in his arm that acted as a cave into his body – it was so deep, a person could see his tendons and veins while looking into it. The infection had entered his bloodstream and he needed IV antibiotics to contain it. He was a young man, maybe 30 years old, but he looked as though he had lived through 100 years of adversity. He was an extremely difficult person to deal with, probably because he was dealing with not having any illegal drugs in his system.

I had been called to the floor where his room was because the nurse managing his case had heard some wheezes from his lungs and thought he could use a breathing treatment. I think the actual reason was the fact that the nurse desperately needed a break from him and his demands. I walked into the room and found him on the bed, sitting up with some help from the five pillows behind his head. His eyes were rolled back, and his limbs were limp. I walked up to the bed and called his name, but he didn't respond. After checking to make sure he was still breathing, I listened to his lungs and discovered that, for once, the nurse was correct. I removed the meds from my pocket and filled the nebulizer cup, plugging it into the oxygen outlet and attaching the other end to the translucent mask. As I slipped the strap over his head, Jimbo's eyelids fluttered and a loud groan emitted from his pale lips.

"What the fuck, man? What is that noise?" Jimbo slowly moved one of his hands and tried to remove the mask from his face. I gently lowered his hand back down to the bed and straightened the mask.

"Hey, calm down. It's just a breathing treatment for your lungs. Just breathe in the mist and you'll feel better."

"Only thing that'll make me feel better is a bundle. Where am I , anyway? And who the fuck are you?" Jimbo made a half-hearted attempt to grab my ass, which I easily avoided.

"You're in the hospital, and I'm a respiratory therapist. What's the last thing you remember?"

"Cooking that cup full of pills into powder and shooting it up here," Jimbo pointed to the surgically placed IV line in his neck. His veins had been so abused by his drug use he needed that IV line to receive any fluids. Of course, it was only supposed to be used by the medical staff. He couldn't possibly have used it himself . . . could he?

"Jimbo, did you cook those pills in this room?" I felt his pulse, which was slow and thready. He had fallen back onto the bed and his eyes were half-closed. I looked around the room and noticed that his dinner tray hadn't been returned. A metal spoon with burnt marks was sitting on the table along with a dirty needle that Jimbo must have reached into the sharps box to get. This was unbelievable, and yet the evidence was right there in front of my eyes. I reached for the call bell and pressed it firmly. A few seconds later the nurse arrived.

"Well, what did I tell you? Trouble breathing." She stood there in her fake triumph, hands on her hips as if she were scolding a child.

"And the reason he's having trouble is because he took all his oral meds and shot them into his PICC line, you moron. Look at him – we'll be lucky if he doesn't stop breathing all together. Don't tell me you gave him a big cup full of pills and just left him here all alone. Have you lost your mind?" As I was chastising her, the nurse had come closer to the bed and dropped her former arrogant stance. She took a flashlight and peeled open his eyelids, shining the light directly into his eyeballs. Jimbo didn't budge, and the nurse turned off the flashlight.

"Well, how was I supposed to know he'd do anything except swallow them?"

"The fact that he's a drug addict that uses needles should have tipped you off. Call the quick response team and make sure he's not left alone in this room." I stormed out of the doorway and picked up the phone in the hall to call the head therapist. He should know to prepare a bed in the ICU for this poor ignorant man.

Callback

The phone again – I had put it on vibrate, but it still woke me up. I groggily reached for it and looked at the ID; it was Sid, my date from the other night. I had not expected to hear from him again, regardless of the cheers I received from Hannah and Thia when I told them about our date. I almost regretted going out with him at all, because I had enjoyed myself so much. Romance was the last thing I needed to deal with, but it was tempting to think that this time it might actually work out.

"Hello?"

"Woke you up, huh? I had to take a chance seeing as how you never gave me your schedule the other day." Sid sounded sleepy as well.

"That's fine. What are you up to?"

"Just got back from Philly last night. I was filling in on bass for a friend that hurt his hand last week on his day job. Construction is a hard gig." Sid paused, and I heard him inhale deeply. A respiratory therapist dating a hardcore smoker; this was an irony I enjoyed. "So, are you up for another date, or do you have a shift tonight?"

I sat up and rubbed my eyes. This was a question I had not been prepared for; what should I say? It's true, I had a very good time and he seemed like an extremely easy-going guy. On the other hand, this might develop into something serious. Was I ready for that?

"I have to work tonight, and my schedule's a little crazy for the rest of the week. How about I call you when I have a better handle on things and we'll make some plans. Sound good?" I felt a tad guilty about putting him off, but I needed time to think.

"That's good for me. I'm in no shape to go anywhere tonight anyway. Give me a shout soon."

"Yeah, I will."

"OK."

I put the phone down and looked at the clock. Two-fifteen. I could manage another couple hours before I had to get up and shower. I laid back down and closed my eyes but sleep seemed impossible. I was too nervous and excited about tomorrow night. I sat up and dialed Hannah – she would love to hear all about this.

Monthly Meeting

After I hung up with Hannah, I took a quick shower and grabbed a snack. I almost forgot that I had to go in early to attend a department meeting These meetings are not something I look forward to, but everyone is required to go once a month. Usually, the topics are mundane and uninteresting; budgeting, statistics, that sort of thing. I'm not sure what the agenda will be today, but I hope I don't fall asleep.

I walk into the break room and grab a seat in the corner near the back. There's only one other person here, and I have never seen her before. She's dressed in a brightly colored business suit and bedecked with the usual outrageous amount of gold jewelry that goes along with being in the corporate world. This must be some kind of salesperson who's been invited to demonstrate a new piece of technology we'll be forced to use without the proper amount of training. She shoots a wan smile my way and then continues to set up her equipment with the air of someone who is attempting to inspire confidence. Not much hope of that, I'm afraid.

Everyone files in and finds a chair, and then the management team arrives. This consists of seven people, and that doesn't include the enormous amount of "administrative" staff that also occupy the offices. The therapists that do the real work upstairs with the patients cannot figure out why we need so many non-clinical positions. But, as in every big corporation, the workers aren't entitled to any explanations. Today I notice that only Todd and Amy have joined us, and this is a bit confusing.

The department director, Amy, takes her place at the front of the room. Amy has been at the hospital for forty years, and she has been the respiratory director for thirty of those years. I find her to be a level-headed and reasonable person. She is always available to listen to a person with a problem, and she seems genuinely interested in finding solutions to these problems. Today, however, I see a difference in her demeanor. She is stiff and tense; she looks over the crowd as though she is about to face a firing squad. She looks at Todd, who nods at her before taking a seat at the front of the room. Then she clears her throat and begins speaking in a calm but wavering voice.

"Welcome everyone. I know that we usually start with routine business, but today I have some news that may shock you. I would like to get it out of the way before we continue with anything else." Amy takes a deep breath and straightens the lapels of her gray business suit. "A few days ago, I was forced to terminate the employment of a person who has been here for twenty years. I'm sure you'll all agree that Tom will be sorely missed." There is a general gasp as everyone in the room absorbs the news. This is a serious blow, and all of the people around me are shocked. Tom was loved and admired not just by me, but by everyone in the department. I had learned so much just by working with him, and he had saved the ass of almost every person sitting in the room.

Amy pauses for a few minutes to allow everyone in the room to absorb the news, and then she continues. "I know that most of you will not agree with the decision that the management team has made regarding Tom, but it's all for the best. I cannot go into any details, but I assure you that this is the best thing for the respiratory team overall." There is a general buzzing as people turn to one another, whispering questions and shrugging their shoulders. Amy, however, is nonplussed by the noise and actually appears relieved. She paces across the room, picks up a thick stack of papers, and begins to pass them around. "Now that we have that unpleasant business taken care of, let's move on to the agenda at hand today. This packet that you're being given is a cost analysis of our department revenue over the past year. As you know, things are tough all over and the hospital is no exception. The higher ups want value for the wages they pay out, and they are determined to cut everything that isn't absolutely necessary."

I flip through the packet, looking at pie charts and projection statements. This doesn't seem like something I should be interested in – my job is taking care of patients, not worrying about the profit margin. I can hear the grumbles and groans of my co-workers, and I know they feel the same way I do.

" I can tell that this is not the subject matter you were expecting to discuss today, but there is a reason why I'm telling you this." Amy stands at the front of the room with her hands on her hips. "Money is tight everywhere, and we are facing massive cuts. The administration is anticipating that Medicare cuts are going to be brutal, and unfortunately we are one of the gray areas of reimbursement. I'm here to tell you that if we do not get our act together we'll be the first department to start instituting layoffs.

" That dirty word – layoffs. Everyone looks around and then down at the floor – this is very bad news. The economy is horrible, and now it seems the healthcare field is immune no longer.

"In order to avoid this, I have come up with a solution that I think everyone will be pleased with." Amy takes another stack of papers and begins to hand them out. "This is a revised copy of the schedule we use on a monthly basis. As you can see, the schedule will be done on a biyearly basis from this point on. And as of now, everyone will be working eight-hour shifts instead of twelve. This will allow us to utilize all staff members to their hourly potential and bring down our overtime budget to near zero."

Amy is smiling as she says this, but her smile fades as she notices the looks on the faces of the people in the room. Shock, anger, confusion – and not one grin.

"So we'll all be working one to two shifts extra per week? I just want to make sure that I understand this." Shirley stands up as she states her question, and everyone turns to look at her. She is a young, perky woman who started working here a year ago, and she was fresh out of school at the time. She is a single mother with two children, and she took this job because she was promised a three-day schedule.

"Well, I don't think you should look at it that way, Shirley. I think that this . . . "

"How exactly am I supposed to look at it, Amy? I'm not trying to be rude, but this is going to change the life of everyone here. One or two extra days a week may not seem like a lot to you, but . . . "

"How will your life change if you get laid off, Shirley? Huh?" Amy's face had gotten red, and she was pacing in little circles at the front of the room. "Every job in this room is in jeopardy, and that includes mine. The administration wants more bang for their buck, and this is the way they want to try to get it. I suggest that you try to get used to this as the way it's going to be. If not, then I guess you'll have no choice but to seek other employment. Are there any other questions?"   Amy's face relaxed and she returned to her normal demeanor. "I'm sure we'll all be able to adjust to our new situation in no time. And now I have Faith here from the DME company . . ."

"Uh, I have a question. Why isn't the rest of the management team here?" Evan asked from the back of the room.

Amy's head swiveled back and her face reflected panic. "I was going to address that after the demonstration, but since you asked we can discuss it now." She motioned for the representative to sit down, but she ducked into the hallway instead. Even this woman, who had never met any of us in her life, knew that this conversation was not going to be pleasant.

"We have had some vacancies since last month's meeting, and I didn't want to just tell you in an email. It seems so impersonal," Amy said while pacing back and forth across the carpet. "There were a few, um, resignations in the past two weeks, most of them involving . . ."

"Who resigned, Amy?" Shirley asked. Amy stopped walking and looked down at the floor.

"There are three managers that resigned, and one team leader," Todd said, getting up from his seat and joining Amy in the center of the room. "They had all received offers of employment from other hospitals, and they felt that it was time to move on."

"And how long were you going to keep us in the dark?" Shirley's face had taken on a reddish hue, and her forehead was prickly with sweat. "I don't think that's a good way of handling it. We don't even get a chance to say goodbye or talk to them, and they're gone?"

"I have their contact information in my office, and you are welcome to it at any time," Todd said. He gripped his hands together and took a deep breath before continuing. "We weren't going to keep you in the dark, but such a mass exodus is disturbing and Amy and I were discussing how to present it to the rest of the department."

"Are those positions going to be filled?" Evan asked. There was a general rumbling amongst the other therapists in the room as the question hung unanswered in the air for a few minutes.

"We're not sure," Amy said after clearing her throat. "The administration is not sure that having so many management positions in this department is the best way to utilize budget money. There's going to be a hospital-wide budget meeting in a few months, and the final decision will be made then."

"Until then I will be the only manager here," Todd said, while walking to the front of the room. "Amy has so many things on her plate as it is, so I will be the main contact for respiratory. Concerns, questions, discipline problems . . . I will be handling them myself until further notice." He seemed to puff out his chest as he said this, and looked around the room to make sure everyone understood what he was saying. Amy made no other comment and took a seat in the back of the room. The therapists looked at each other and then down at the floor, seeming to know that surrender was the best option.

"Now let's bring Faith back in here for our in-service, OK?" Todd said and then stepped into the hall.

Shirley leaned over and whispered in my ear, "Wow, this sucks, doesn't it?"

I had no choice but to mutely nod my head in utter disbelief. Three managers, one team leader, and Tom – all in two weeks. There had to be something under the surface that was going on – I knew, however, that I was not one of the privileged few that would receive that information. I looked up and saw Todd walking into the room with Faith. He took a seat a few placed away from me, and gave me a look of sheer triumph.

I was headed for trouble.

Spy Games

"Are you sure this is a good idea?" Evan asked as he edged his way down the hall toward Todd's office. "Maybe we should just leave it alone."

"There are so many things I could say to counter that comment. 'I was just following orders' is one that comes to mind." I turned to face Evan. "Don't you want to know what's going on around here?"

"Well, yes, of course, but . . ."

"Then please go in there and ask if you can have Linda's contact info, and I'll do the rest. If I ask Todd, he'll know what's up. I want to get the truth out of someone, and unfortunately this seems to be the only way to do it. Just trust me, OK? I've been here a lot longer than you have."

Evan looked at me and then smiled. "You're the only person here besides Tom that ever helped me out when I first came here, so I'll do it. " He walked down the hall and ducked into Todd's open office door. I walked down the hall and took a seat near the timeclock. I have never been a patient person, but in this case I would be willing to wait for several hours to receive the information I needed.

It was only a few minutes before Evan came back, grinning. "Here," he said, handing me a piece of scrap paper with a phone number and email address scribbled on it. "He didn't even ask me what I wanted it for. It looks like he's plotting which new office is going to be his." He gave me a quizzical look and sat down next to me. "I must say, I am curious about why everyone left so suddenly, but what good is it going to do the rest of us who are left here?"

"I honestly don't know, Evan," I muttered while watching the other therapists file out the back door. "But I do know that I can't just sit back and accept what these people are telling me. I need to find out the real reason everyone left, and I know that Linda will tell me. Especially now that she's safely out of here."

"OK. Tell me when you find anything out. I gotta punch out so I'll see you." I waved at him as he swiped the timeclock with his ID and joined Shirley at the back door.

I looked again at the paper that Evan had procured for me. The phone number and email address were connected to a hospital that was clear across the state. Linda apparently had seen something noone else was aware of and had arranged a parachute for herself. I needed to find out if I should prepare one too. I looked at my watch – 8 pm. OK, not too late. I took my cell phone out of my pocket and dialed the number. After four rings, voice mail picked up.

"Hello, you have reached the desk of Linda, respiratory coordinator. If this is an emergency please dial zero. Otherwise, leave your message after the tone and I'll get back to you shortly." I waited until the tone stopped. "Hey, Linda, we just got out of the department meeting and found out you left. Everyone here is shocked and I guess I'm calling to find out what's going on. You have my number so call me." Linda and I had known each other for a long time, so long that we didn't need to leave our names when we called each other. That's why this was so disconcerting. I didn't wait for her to call me back – I had to get upstairs. But as I swung the door open to the stairwell, I found myself hoping her call would come sooner rather than later.

A Way to Make Things Better

The room is full of people. Damn, I should have gotten here earlier. I look around for a seat and there are only open tables in the front. I walk quickly down the aisle of the auditorium and take a seat two spaces away from an older woman in scrubs. She throws me a wan smile and then looks to the front of the room, where a large projection screen is being rolled down by two women in business suits. I recognize one of them as a higher-up in the Human Resources Department. The other woman has a visitor's badge stuck onto her lapel. She seems very stressed, and keeps blowing a piece of hair from her forehead. She's not the only one in the room who doesn't seem to want to be here.

This is a mandatory two-hour seminar entitled "A Way to Make Things Better." I have waited until the last possible moment to take this class, if it can be called that, and I am extremely angry that I have to waste my time in this manner. The seminar was created by the upper management to "train" the employees to treat patients as though they're high-end clients in a four star hotel. I'm completely expecting to receive printed handouts on the best take-out in the area and where the best prostitutes can be located. After all, who wants to be bored and sick in a hospital when you can have your every whim catered to?

I settle into the uncomfortable chair and wait for the show to begin. A few more people wander in and sit down at my table, and then the two women running the seminar step up to a wooden podium. As one of them begins to speak, the air is filled with the familiar sound of audio feedback, and the room bursts into laughter. As we all quiet down, the microphone is adjusted and the real work begins. We are shown a video (stressed as "unscripted") of a patient discussing his outstanding experience at our facility. The video is a detailed description of the perfect hospital visit; private room, caring staff, clean facilities. There is no mention of medical mistakes, rescheduled tests or inexperienced residents. Our newly minted logo caps off the surreal experience, looming above us on the screen.

The lights are turned up and several happy nappers are shocked into consciousness. The two suited women start passing out copies of the "new" values we as employees will be expected to embody. As I look over the pages I have to stifle a laugh – these are values that everyone in this room already practices. After about five minutes, we are led through a series of supposedly thought-provoking exercises. The people at my table are as irritated as I am, and we half-heartedly participate. There are several theoretical situations regarding patients and staff that we have to read aloud and write comments about. One involves a lost visitor, another speaks to patient confidentiality. At the bottom of the page is a scenario in which a co-worker is seen speaking on a cell phone in a clinical area. We are told by the suited women that the "right" answer is to confront the co-worker and tell her/him to put away the phone. I look around my table and see that my opinion of this answer is echoed in the brain of every other person here – now I'm going to be expected to be an extension of the long arm of management. Every staff member will have to become a snitch and a spy in order to receive the measly raise we expect at the end of the year.

At the end of the seminar, the exits are clogged – no one can get out fast enough. The air in the room has become stagnant with frustration and disbelief. Caring for patients in the best way possible isn't enough anymore; now we have to sell ourselves and our hospital as if we're competing for a government contract. Luckily, I'm familiar with the auditorium and slip out a side exit hidden behind a curtain. I'm done with this bullshit, and I have much better things to do with my time.

Written Warning

I went home after the class and grabbed a few hours of sleep. Then I had to get back up and come back for my regular shift – it seems like I spend more time at work than I do anywhere else. As I walked into the department I could see Todd pacing in the hallway. Anyone can tell that we have a bad history. I'm pretty sure he'd like to drop me off a rooftop, and I know for a fact that I wouldn't blink an eye if he were flattened by a truck. We don't speak unless we have to, and it looked like this was one of those times. When he saw me he stopped and motioned for me to follow him into his office.

I walked into the small box of a space and sat down in a very uncomfortable wooden chair perched in front of an oblong desk. I remember each and every time I had to sit here, and pleasant memories are not what came to mind.

Todd walked in behind me and sat down in his cushioned swivel chair behind the desk. He extracted a piece of paper from a pile to the left of his elbow and placed it carefully in front of me. I recognized the form immediately – it was a written warning.

"Do you know why I have to give you this?" Todd leaned back in his chair and gave me an expectant look.

"No, Todd, but I'm sure you're about to tell me. What did I do now?" Todd's face flushed and he sat forward.

"I don't think this is the time for you to be flippant. There was a patient complaint about you and Amy and I have decided to give you this warning based on what we heard. Do you remember last week when you were covering the 5th floor?"

"Yes I do. And I'm sure I remember the patient. He requested a breathing treatment at 3 am and I determined from my assessment that he didn't need one. He seemed very angry that he couldn't get what he wanted and threatened to have me fired. Is that the patient you're referring to?"

Todd got up and handed me the paper. "Yes, that is the patient. Why didn't you give him the treatment? He asks for one every night around the same time and has never been refused before."

"Because he didn't need one. He wasn't short of breath, he was pissed off and bored. He gets a treatment every night because all of the other therapists are afraid of this very situation happening to them. But I'm not." I stood up and handed the paper back to Todd. "You can do whatever you like with this warning but you'll be doing it without my signature. I am a professional, and I think I can tell when someone needs medication. I stand by my decision and my flowsheet will prove it. " I turned to leave but Todd moved forward and blocked my path to the door.

"That's it? That's all you have to say about this? Let me show you something." He grabbed a stack of papers and shook them in his hand. "These are resumes and applications. There's at least 20 of them here. If you decide to walk out of here without signing the warning, I may be forced to replace you with one of these people. You should take a hint from the meeting." He put the papers down and stood unwavering with a smug smirk pasted onto his face. I walked around him and turned the knob on the door.

"I'm sure that Human Resources will be very interested to hear what you've just told me. Don't' make me go downstairs and talk to them after my shift, Todd. I've never been the kind of person to make waves, but if you're going to threaten me I might not have a choice." I leaned into his face. "You and I both know that patient is a whiny, entitled ass who likes to make trouble. He's miserable that he's sick and he wants everyone else to be miserable too. You disappoint me, Todd. You don't seem like a corporate puppet, but I guess you've turned into a lackey like all the other sycophants here. I suppose that's what happens when you're the only manager ." Todd's face turned a shade of purple I've only seen in a child's marker box, and he moved slowly toward his desk as I left.

Death Trials

The meeting with Todd had shaken me despite my cool exterior, and I had to stop in the restroom to get some perspective. As I stood in front of the mirror practicing the deep breathing Larry taught me my beeper went off. I looked at the number and suppressed the urge to bash my head into the wall. It was the hospice unit calling – never a good sign.

I walked into the office and called the extension. A panicked nurse answered and began babbling at top speed so it took me a minute to even figure out which patient she was talking about. Eventually I identified the problem; Eddie, a 45-year old man infected with HIV and hepatitis, was having significant difficulty breathing. He had contracted pneumonia while in the hospital, and his already fragile health had quickly declined from there. Despite his young age, he had signed a no-code order that prevented anyone from resuscitating him, and that limited our choices. He had been wearing an oxygen mask for days and that had seemed to help, but now there was a crisis with his lungs. The antibiotics were becoming ineffective, and the infection was slowly killing him. I tried to talk to the nurse but she was still panicked.

"I don't know what to do for him. He's panting and hanging over the bed. What should I do?" I could hear her breathing heavily into the phone, and I hoped I wouldn't have two patients when I got up there.

"Does he have any family or friends listed in his chart? If he does, you need to call them and update them on his condition. Is the doc there yet?"

"No, and we paged him four times. The other nurses are calling the ICUs and trying to find out where he is."

"At this point, don't bother. Call a help code over the intercom – if that doesn't put a fire under his ass, nothing will. Oh, and call the nursing supervisor too – we'll need her help."

I hung up the phone and speed walked to the elevator. By the time I got up to the room, everyone required had been assembled. The nursing supervisor was at the desk with a phone held to her ear and waved at me. The nurse taking care of the patient, two male aides, a PCA, and of course the white-robed doctor were standing at the entrance to Eddie's room. This doctor looked about as old as a tenth-grader, and was peering into the room nervously.

"Excuse me, please." I shoved through the crowd and starting hooking up a nebulizer treatment to the oxygen. Eddie was flailing around in the bed, looking wildly from side to side at all the people that were beginning to file into the small room.

"Who are all these people? I don't want this right now – everyone please get out." He flapped his arms up and down in what would have been a humorous gesture if the situation wasn't so dire. "Hey, you . . . " Eddie grabbed the sleeve of my scrub shirt and hauled me up into his sweat-soaked face. "I know you. I've seen you in here at night checking on me. Can't you get rid of these assholes for me?" He lost his strength and fell back against the damp pillows. "Where's my mother? She was supposed to be here tonight, and that's what I've been waiting for. Where the fuck is she? MAMA!" The sudden scream took everyone by surprise, and most of the staff scattered out into the hallway.

I finished setting up the nebulizer and slipped the mask over Eddie's face. The medicinal steam enveloped his head and rose into the air. He turned and looked my way. A sweet smile appeared on his lips as he stared.

"Oh good. Mama, you're finally here. I've been waiting for you to come." Eddie reached out to take my hand and squeezed it. "I couldn't leave without saying goodbye to you, and now you're here. What a relief." His face relaxed, and he leaned back into his bed.

The nurse who was taking care of Eddie stopped preparing the morphine drip the doctor had ordered. "But Eddie, don't you know who this is? This isn't . . . " I made a sharp cutting motion with the hand Eddie wasn't holding.

"Don't you listen to her, Eddie. It's me, Mama, and I'm here with you right now. All the nice people here have told me what a hard time you're having. Are you in a lot of pain? Because if you are, your nurse is about to give you some medicine that will make you feel better. Will you let her give it to you?" I motioned to the nurse, and she began to hook up the drip to the IV. Eddie didn't protest, and I continued to hold his hand.

"Oh, Mama I'm so tired. I don't think I have enough energy to make it one more day. Do you think it would be OK if I rested for a little while? I'm just so happy to have you here. I've been so afraid." Eddie closed his eyes and began to whisper words of love and admiration for the woman he called his mother, and I sat by his side to listen.

After a few minutes, Eddie stopped talking and seemed to fall asleep. I gently took the hand I was holding and put it down by his side. As I was tiptoeing out of the room, the doctor entered and began asking questions in a loud clinical voice.

"Eddie, do you feel better now that the nurse has started the morphine? Are you still having trouble breathing? Eddie?" He leaned down to check his pulse and I tapped him on the shoulder.

"He's very comfortable right now, and since he doesn't want anything else done I think we should leave him alone."

"I don't see you leaving the room. What makes you so special?" He looked at me with a superior smirk. Apparently his nervous exterior earlier was a front for the arrogant prick he really was. "What are you, a respiratory therapist? What gives you the right to tell me what to do? I tell you what to do, remember?"

"Look, if you want to pull rank that's fine. I would just ask that you do it later. Can't you see this man is dying?" I pointed to the monitor bolted above the bed. "His pulse and respiratory rate are slowing down. He's delusional. Are you prepared to sit here and watch him die? Because I am. It's the very least I can do for a human being who hasn't got one person in the world that will stand by him." I stood up straight and moved closer to him. "Besides, he thinks I'm his mother."

"What? He must really be delusional. What do you care? He's just a junkie and a loser. Everyone in this building knows it. He doesn't even deserve to have the bed he's lying in. So you go ahead and waste your time pretending to be his long-lost mama. I hope you're not neglecting your other duties." He turned to leave the room, and then swiveled back on his heel. "And you're damn right, I will be pulling rank on you later. Who's your manager? What's his name so I can go file a complaint right now?" He pulled a pen and pad out of his pocket and starting writing, but just at that moment the monitor emitted a sharp beep. Eddie's pulse was registering as zero, as was his breathing rate. I walked over to the bed and took Eddie's hand one more time. Then I placed it on the bed and turned around.

"Well, I guess you won't have to worry about wasting any more of your time with this loser junkie. Do you still want to file a complaint, or do you want to spend some time searching for your compassion? You've obviously misplaced it." I brushed past him as he stood there with his mouth agape, shocked that a regular human being would dare question one of the gods of medicine.

The Dog Days of July

I work in a teaching hospital, which means that all kinds of students come through the building to learn their particular trade firsthand with actual patients. Most of the time these students are heavily supervised and the work they perform is examined with care. But there is an exception to this rule – residents. They descend in a cloud of white lab coats every July and spend one year making the kind of mistakes that could get a full-fledged doctor into an ocean of hot water.

These students are unlike any other I've ever seen. They are supervised by an intern and overseen by a staff doctor, but they are given full power over any patient they're assigned to. They write orders, offer advice to other professionals, and run codes in emergency situations. Basically, they are entitled to the same power of a doctor without the full education of one. And the results can be disastrous.

During one of my shifts, I was called to the 10th floor to assist in a code involving a woman in labor. The resident had not listened to the patient when she told him that her epidural had not been successful. She was still feeling pain and was having trouble pushing the baby out. After 4 hours of pushing, the resident decided it was time for an emergency c-section. As she was being wheeled into the OR, the patient protested that she needed something else to eliminate the pain. When the OR nurse tested an area with a pin to make sure it was numb, the patient reacted. While the resident was scratching his head trying to decide what to do, the patient lost consciousness. In the time it took to anesthetize and stabilize her, the patient had suffered massive blood loss. Both the baby and the mother ended up in separate ICUs , each with their very own breathing tubes and ventilators. And the resident? He went home after his 48-hour shift to return after two days of rest. There was no investigation, no complaints, and that resident went on to become a full-fledged obstetrician. Now let's think about this – if you were a pregnant woman, would you want a doctor caring for you that had made a mistake as monumental as this?

Never mind; it's a trick question. Why? Because you would never know the mistake had been made in the first place. The patients and their family members are placated by nursing supervisors and suits who promise to get to the bottom of the problem. If that doesn't satisfy, then the big guns are called in. Lawyers and ethics committees are informed of the situation, and then the paperwork and subterfuge begins. Legal cases against hospitals can take years, and in that time the mistake is buried between subpoenas. Noone ever knows exactly what happened, and in time it's forgotten.

Except by the patient. Assuming they're still alive.

Training Manual

The day after my patient Eddie died, I walked into the department to attend a training session. It was mandatory, and I had waited until the last minute to sign up. I sat down at the long table with a few other stragglers and waited while the representative from the medical equipment company finished setting up his display. There was a stack of handouts in the middle of the table, and I grabbed one from the top. I flipped through twenty or so pages of graphs and charts without grasping what the training would actually involve.

"OK, everyone ready? My name is Timothy and today I'll be training you to operate the ES 200 ventilator. Our company is extremely excited about this new product, and I hope you will be too. Now, if you'll please turn to page two of your packet, we'll begin." The rep, a bouncy man who looked like he had just graduated from middle school a month ago, began to lead us through the packet we had received. I looked around at the three people with me in the room, and I was relieved to see faces of confusion. Shirley, the single mom who had spoken up in the department meeting, raised her hand.

"Um, Timothy, is it? The information you've given us so far is very interesting but it doesn't really have anything to do with direct patient care. Can you tell me what kind of person this machine is intended for?"

Timothy wrinkled his brow and smiled. "Well, I don't really work with patients per say, so I think that would be a question to ask your manager."

"Has our manager been trained on this machine yet?" Shirley asked. "I don't think this training was mandatory for him, and in any case he won't be working with it. I don't mean to be rude, but I thought this training was to get a true understanding of the equipment. How is that possible if you can't even tell me when to use it?" She shifted back in her seat and gave Timothy an expectant look.

"Um, that's a very good question and you have every right to ask it. Who else in the room feels the same way?" Timothy looked nervously around as the rest of the therapists, myself included, raised their hands. He broke into a sweat and began wringing his hands.

"You know what? Todd happens to be in his office right now, and I'm just going to have a chat with him about your concerns. How about we take a 15-minute break?" Timothy scampered down the hall and we looked at each other with amused grins.

"An infant. Where do they get these guys?" Shirley poked me in the ribs and shook her purse in my face. "Wanna go with me while I have my breathing treatment?" I nodded and followed her out into the hall. We took the elevator to the ground floor and walked outside to the unofficial smoking area – a dilapidated shack formerly used by security located near two enormous dumpsters. It was on the edge of hospital property, and the dumpsters hid the shack from view. Shirley lit up and offered me one, but I shook my head.

"I still can't understand why you smoke when you're a respiratory therapist. How can you do that to your body when you know what it can do to you?" I leaned against a post while Shirley inhaled deeply from her "treatment". Of course, my question seemed hypocritical but I was curious as to what her answer would be. I knew what my motivation was, but I wanted to know her reasons.

"Well, there's lots of reasons, really. I enjoy the irony, for one. Who would guess that a therapist is out here smoking?" Two other people in the shack raised their hands and Shirley gave them the finger, laughing. "OK, fine, so it's not a big secret. But I'm also ensuring my future employment. I can give myself nebulizers and set up my own oxygen when the time comes." She paused to take another hit off her cigarette and blew the smoke out languidly. "But here's the most important reason. How else am I supposed to relieve stress? It's not like I can show up for my shift drunk. Sometimes this is the only thing that keeps me from choking someone." She crushed out her butt in the ashtray and waved to the other two smokers, who nodded. "Our fifteen minutes are up, cupcake. Shall we?" She linked arms with me and we walked back to the department.

Todd was standing in the corner of the room with Timothy, engaged in a soft conversation punctuated with sweeping arm movements. He turned when Shirley and I walked in, giving us a look that would wilt lettuce. Timothy left the room swiftly and Todd stood over the table.

"So, Shirley, let me get this straight. You aren't satisfied with the in-service?"

Shirley looked down at the floor, then back up into Todd's face. "No, Todd, I'm not. Timothy seems like a very nice and well-intentioned person, and he has a wonderful grasp of the machinery itself. But that's not what I'm supposed to be learning here. My expertise is patient care, not mechanics. If that's what I was interested in, I wouldn't have gone to respiratory school. So now that I see Timothy's gone, are you going to tell me which patients I should use this on and why?" She sat down in her seat and gave Todd an expectant look.

Todd turned from the table to compose himself and saw the other two therapists attending the training session standing in the doorway. Todd turned back to the table and picked up one of the packets.

"This is all you need to know about this machine, Shirley. How to operate it. You're not a doctor."

"And that's just it, Todd. The doctors who write the orders don't have a clue about any of this stuff. They rely on us to tell them which machines, which drugs, which therapy to order. We tell them, and they write it. If all I know is how to plug it in, what good am I?" Shirley stood up and pushed back her chair. "I will not be using this unless I'm fully trained. It's not safe and someone might get hurt." She walked past Todd and paused in the doorway. "You know, Todd, this seems to be the way we're trained on every new piece of high-priced crap that comes through the door. Maybe that's how a patient got a punctured lung last week? I don't know . . . just seems like too much of a coincidence to me." I resisted the urge to fist-pump Jersey style as she flounced to the time clock and punched out.

Fucking right.

Heat Wave

After that nasty performance by Todd and Shirley, I could hardly wait to leave the building. I had four days off, a stretch of time that is nearly impossible to achieve these days. As I was driving home I was thinking about all the things I had planned when I felt the top of my head being to itch uncontrollably. This was happening a lot lately, and I was getting a little worried. I released my hold on the steering wheel with my right hand and scratched the area, and as I pulled my hand away I noticed a trail of hair wrapped around my index finger. I looked at it carefully as I paused at an intersection – fuck! It was a small wad of hair, but it had taken no effort for it to fall out. What was this all about? Did I have cancer? Follicle reduction? A whole plethora of ideas floated through my head as I parked my car and walked into my apartment building. I dropped my keys on the hallway floor and bent down to pick them up, swearing to myself. As I grabbed the key ring I noticed a black Doc Marten boot by my eye. I straightened up and came face to face with Sid, my one time date from last week. Great. He was grinning from ear to ear as he leaned against the doorway to my apartment and was holding a large paper bag.

"Hey there. You haven't been returning my phone calls. Is that normal or are you avoiding me?"

"I've been really busy at work. How did you know which number I was? I don't remember telling you."

"You didn't. Your friend Hannah was kind enough to supply me with it when I called her." He continued to grin and shifted his weight from one foot to the other. I grimaced and reminded myself to call Hannah later. I had a list of obscene names already forming in my brain.

"Well, while you're here you might as well come in." I stepped past him to unlock my door and held it open as he entered. He looked around with an appraising glance, then set the paper bag down on the kitchen counter.

"So, do you have any plans for tonight? I was hoping we could have that second date after you blew me off."

I set down my work bag and walked slowly over to the refrigerator for a drink. "I didn't blow you off, I had to work. Would you like something?" I asked as I held out a pitcher of iced coffee. "I don't have much in here but you're welcome to it." I turned to get another glass when I felt Sid's hand on the small of my back. It sent shivers up my neck and I turned around slowly. I could feel his gaze travel across my body like a ray of hidden sunlight, and the shivers moved languidly down my spine.

"I've been thinking about you ever since that night we went out. You have such a brittle shell but I know if I could just make a crack in it . . ." Sid's hand moved downward, and I broke away.

"Sid, I don't think we know each other well enough to have this conversation. We've had one date, and already you want to 'crack my shell'. This is ridiculous." I took my glass and sat down in my rocking chair by the large window. "I've been married twice. Did you know that? Did any of my friends tell you that?" I shifted my feet to move the chair back and forth, refusing to look at Sid. "I'm sure that once you get to know me, you'll run screaming from the room never to be seen again. And quite frankly, I'd rather avoid the inevitable conclusion."

Sid crossed over to where I was sitting and knelt down in front of me. "OK, let me get this straight. You know for a fact that we wouldn't be good together and you'd rather not waste your time? Is that it? Cuz if it is, you and I both know that's bullshit. What are you so afraid of? Maybe I can remove the enormous stick that's up your ass and you could breathe for once in your life." He took my hand and stroked it. "I'm not asking to marry you. And by the way, I've been married twice too. Not something I tell many people, but I think you'd understand where I'm coming from. All I'm asking for is some time. Can you spare me that? It might actually be worth it. For both of us."

I stopped rocking and looked into his eyes. They mirrored me in the deep pools of brown color, and I saw a tired and frustrated woman. A woman barely clinging to life and hating every minute of it. Is this what I wanted to be? Or could this man be the key out of the hole I'd dug for myself?

"I still don't understand why this is so important to you. Don't you have girls throwing themselves at you every time you play? I can imagine it in my head right now – ripped leather thongs hanging from the neck of your bass."

Sid chuckled and stayed where he was, keeping a firm grasp on my hand. "I don't know. I just feel like I've known you for a long time and it would be a mistake to walk away. I don't feel that way very often, so maybe it's important that I pay attention. C'mon, let me buy you dinner – you look hungry. I promise I'll keep my hands to myself – unless you have some panties you'd like to be rid of?"

I repressed a smile and allowed myself to feel my hand in his. It felt natural, normal. Maybe this was something I shouldn't ignore, either. "OK Sid. Let's go out. It's not like I have anything to do tonight anyway. And who knows? Maybe you can teach me how to have fun again." I stood up and walked around him toward the bedroom. "Do you mind waiting while I change?"

Sid took my spot in the rocking chair and started flipping through a magazine on the side table. "Nope. Some things are worth waiting for." He winked at me, and I felt myself blushing.

I disappeared into my room and tried to suppress a huge smile.

Covert Ops

"Hello?" I juggled the phone to my ear as I attempted to unlock my door. Sid had just dropped me off and it was pretty late. I hadn't bothered to check the caller ID to see who it was, and I was curious. Besides, late calls usually meant trouble, and I wanted to deal with it as soon as possible.

"Hey there troublemaker. How's it going?" Linda's voice rang out, and I was so relieved I dropped my keys.

"Hi! Why are you calling me so late, you weirdo?"

"You forget how long I've known you. You work nights and you never sleep. So, what do you want to know? Whatever it is, I'll tell you."

I finally unlocked my door and walked into my apartment, dumping my backpack on the nearest chair. "Well, first of all, why did you leave without telling anyone? Without telling me?"

Linda sighed into the phone and paused before answering. "I had no choice. I couldn't give away my plans. I've been looking for another position for six months - you know how brutal the job market is these days. And once I secured the job, I wanted to start right away. I'm sure you know that I refused to give the 'required' four weeks notice, and so did everyone else that left. It was a matter of survival."

I took off my shoes and sat down on the floor. "Is it really that gruesome? I mean, everyone's miserable but that's not a radical change. What's going on that most of the management team left so suddenly?"

" I said that I'd tell you whatever you wanted to know, and I will. But if anyone asks you where you came by the info, I'd appreciate it if you left my name out of it."

"No worries. Now spill it." I was starting to get worried, and a number of outrageous ideas fluttered through my head. But none of them even compared to what I was about to hear.

"Amy is finally planning to retire, and HR has Todd on the top of their list to replace her. The rest of the management team didn't agree with this logic, and we all decided to try to think of an alternative. None of us was interested in the position, and so we all went to Tom as a group to convince him to apply."

"So what happened?"

Linda coughed and then continued. "He gave it some thought. Amy's not retiring for at least a year, maybe more, so he had the time. After about six weeks, he went down to HR and put in for the job. Todd found out he had competition, and somehow got rid of Tom. After that, we all jumped ship. I was lucky I got the job offer when I did – a few of the people that left are high and dry at the moment. But we all agreed that if Todd gained control, the department was as good as gone and we didn't want to shoulder any of that responsibility."

I rubbed my eyes as I felt a first-class migraine start to emerge behind my forehead. Could this really be the whole truth? It seemed so fantastical, but this was Linda I was talking to. She was a straight shooter who never minced words – making up a story like this would be completely out of character for her. "OK, this is really incredible to hear so I'm going to have to ask you some questions. Why wouldn't anyone other than Tom and Todd want that job? It seems to me it would be a great accomplishment."

"Noone wanted to try to straighten out the mess it's all become. Some of us have been in the field for twenty years or more – who wants that kind of hassle that late in their career? And it's not as if there's anyone in that place willing to cooperate with us. Nursing sees us as a nuisance, and the administration doesn't think we're worth any attention at all. But Tom had other ideas, and he seemed really committed to turning it all around. He was excited, and he's younger. He was more than willing to take it all on, but none of that's going to happen now."

"How did Todd get rid of Tom? Amy really liked him."

"I never found out. The day after Tom was fired, Todd held a meeting to tell us. It was all presented to us in very vague terms, and none of our questions were answered. Amy wasn't even there, and she wasn't willing to discuss the situation with any of us. It wasn't difficult to see that there was some foul play, but at this point we all had to think of ourselves. I'm a little ashamed to admit it, but I had to take care of myself and so did everyone else." I could hear the trembling in Linda's voice and knew that her guilt would stay with her for a long time. But she was right – she couldn't put herself on the line for someone else if that meant she would ruin her own career.

"Linda, don't feel bad. You did what you had to do, and I don't blame you. And now that I know the story, I'm not mad that you didn't tell me. You couldn't take the chance. Thank you for trusting me - I won't let your name get involved, I promise."

"You're not planning on doing anything about this, are you? I don't think I need to tell you that you're on Todd's shit list." Linda chuckled to herself. "I remember every conversation I ever had with that man about you, and he was always so incensed that you wouldn't bend to his will. You're so lucky I was your manager, but I'm not there anymore."

I got up from the floor and picked up one of the cats that had been rubbing against my legs. I held her to my chest and felt the comforting vibrations echo through my body. "I can take care of myself, Linda. And all of this has to be uncovered."

"Why not just come work for me? I've got a spot reserved for you right now, and I'm authorized to offer you more than what you're making now. You were the best worker I ever had, and I would be honored if you accepted the job."

"I can't do that. You and Tom are my friends, and I really care about the department. At least I know that if Todd manages to get rid of me I'll have a place to go. That's an advantage I have that noone else does right now, and I need to use it to its full extent." I walked into the bedroom and put the cat on the bed, where she curled up and promptly fell asleep. Good idea. "Listen, Linda, I'm really tired so I'm going to bed. I'll call you in a few days and we'll talk again, OK?

"Why are you so tired? Had a hot date?" Linda was now openly laughing, and I knew why. She had seen me through my last divorce and heard my vow never to get involved with a man again. I knew she'd be ecstatic to hear about Sid, but frankly I didn't have the energy and my head was spinning with all the facts I'd just heard.

"Haha. Good night, and I'll talk to you soon." I hung up the phone as she burst into more giggles and sat down. Putting my chin in my hand, I pondered what my next move would be.

Friendly Fire

"Yo, Hannah, get me another margarita while you're up there?" Thia shouted at the table we were sitting at. The girls had decided to take me out for a date debriefing the night after Sid and I had our second date. As usual, the alcohol was flowing freely, and I knew I would again be the taxi service.

Hannah flounced back with the drinks and set them down with a smash. Then she reclaimed her seat by shoving Thia onto the floor and planting herself on the chair. "So, now let's hear all the gory details. Did he kiss you? Or did you do the nasty right there on the floor?"

Thia got herself up from the floor, slapped Hannah on the side of her head and then sat down in another chair. "Hannah, stop being so vulgar. This lady hasn't been laid in years. Did you ever consider the possibility that she's forgotten how to do it?" Thia sat back in her chair and slurped from her glass. Hannah got up and sat in my lap, burying her face in my neck.

"You leave her alone, you bitch." Her voice was muffled and reverberated in my body. "She's having a hard time believing anyone likes her. Just look at the two assholes she married. They both cheated on her and she had no idea it was going on. How would you feel about that?"

"I wouldn't give it a second thought if it were me," Thia replied, putting her glass down on the table. "I would know without a shadow of a doubt that those losers were beneath me and I would move on." She looked at me and tilted her head. "You're not still blaming yourself for that shit, are you? What the hell are you paying that therapist for? He's supposed to be fixing your head not making it worse."

"I can't help but think that it had something to do with me," I said, sipping at my Shirley Temple. I picked a cherry out of the glass and tied a knot in the stem. "I mean, let's examine this. I married two men who were different in every conceivable way, and they both left me for women they were cheating on me with. How is that not my fault?" I popped the cherry in my mouth and chewed it thoughtfully. "Sid is a great guy and very interesting, but how is this time going to be any different? Maybe I should just swear off relationships and join a convent."

"Did you have a good time on the date?" Hannah asked. "Where did he take you?"

"We went to a blues bar and hung out. It was smoky and tiny, and they had the best bar food I've ever had. Then we listened to this awesome band and Sid actually got up and played a few songs with them. I don't think I've ever had a better time with a guy." I could feel myself grinning, and my two friends sat up to take notice.

"Thia, what is that on her face? I don't think I remember seeing her teeth before." Hannah leaned into my face. "Holy shit, I think it's a smile! Wow. I thought you had all your smiling muscles removed years ago."

I pinched Hannah's cheek and moved her into the chair next to me, shaking my head. "C'mon, stop being so melodramatic. I smile all the time."

"Really? Well, honey, I think it's time for an intervention." Thia walked over to where I was sitting and put her hand on the tightly wound bun at the back of my head. "Have you noticed your hair is falling out? Because we have. We didn't want to tell you because we knew it would send you into a tailspin of hypochondria, but I think you need to hear it. You're always tired and have enough bags under your eyes for a trip to Europe. You've been losing weight and you have no good explanation for it. Let's face it, you're falling apart from stress." She put her hand under my chin and gently pulled it up. "We love you and we hate seeing you like this. If Sid can make you feel better, why not go with it? Grab a little bit of happiness and run with it. Besides, if you keep going the way you are, you're not going to be able to take care of anyone else. You'll be too spent."

I stood up and hugged Thia, trying to blink away the tears that were forming in my eyes. "Thank you for your concern. I really appreciate it. But I don't want to be hurt again, and that outweighs everything else." I released Thia and sat back down. "I know I'm stressed out. It's the job. It's getting more and more difficult to walk into work without wanting to vomit. I got written up last week by Todd for some bullshit complaint, and I know I'm on his radar. We have to attend these in services that don't teach us anything, and the management keeps cutting back on the number of therapists per shift. We work our asses off and then get told we can be replaced at any moment. I don't know how much more I can stand, but the economy sucks."

I deliberately left out Linda's story – I didn't want my friends to worry, and I also didn't want them to stage a coup on my behalf.

"Why don't you just find another job? It would be easy for someone like you. You have all that education under your belt and years of experience." Hannah looked at me expectantly and took a sip of her beer. "Any other place would be lucky to have you on their staff."

"See, that's just it. This is the best place to work for a respiratory therapist. The pay is good, and there's more of a variety of patients. Although lately the population has shifted to either old people or addicts detoxing from their drug of choice." I gulped down the rest of my drink and set the glass down with a thump.

Hannah stood up and waved her arms in the air. "Noone is stuck anywhere that they don't want to be. You are such a talented and caring person, and you're wasting yourself in that hellhole." She flounced over to my chair and leaned into my face. "I know. Why don't you work with me? I could get you a job easy."

I suppressed a laugh. "You work in a preschool, Hannah. What kind of experience do I have dealing with other people's brats?"

"None, but it's not like it's rocket science. The money's not as good, but at least you'd be out from under the tyranny of Todd and Amy."

I got up and grabbed the bill from the table. "It's nice of you to offer, but you and I both know that I need to find a different solution." I pulled my wallet out from my back pocket and moved toward the front of the bar. "Now, ladies, if you want a ride home I suggest you pry yourselves from your chairs." Thia and Hannah got up and enveloped me in their arms.

"Don't' worry, hon," Thia whispered into my ear. "We're here for you no matter what you decide to do. But you have to make a decision very soon, or that place is going to kill you from the inside out."

I tried to push back the tears forming in my eyes. "I know, Thia. I know."

Repeat Performance

"So, what are we going to talk about today, hmm?" Larry was sitting at his desk with a rapt expression on his face. "You seem antsier than usual, so what's up?"

I got up from the overstuffed chair I was sitting in and paced back and forth across the carpet. "I feel as though I'm at some kind of proverbial fork in the road of my life, and I can't decide which path to take. Do I stay on the same road and keep accepting what I'm getting, or do I choose the other road and face uncertainty? Either way, I'm not going to be happy."

"Why not? What's wrong with not knowing what's around the corner? It could be something so fabulous it exceeds your wildest dreams."

"Or it could be the worst disaster ever to occur. And I'm not sure I can handle that."

Larry got up from his desk and walked over to the spot where I was standing. He gently directed me toward the bay window and pointed. "What do you see out there?"

I took in the view. "Trees, sidewalks, buildings. Why? What is the point of this?"

"The point," Larry said, turning me back to face him, "is that you're only seeing the surface. What do you think is happening in that apartment building over there? Are there people fighting over money in there? A couple making love? A child happily playing with his toys? With your attitude and lack of insight, you'll never know." He let me go and returned to his desk. "You have been through so much trauma in your life, it's understandable that you would want to cling to anything familiar. But those horrible problems have made you the strong and resilient person you are today. And even if you don't know it, I know that you could withstand any conflict."

"Now that is some of the most articulate bullshit I've ever heard you utter, Larry." I walked back over to my chair and perched on the arm. "I'm a small piece of machinery in a vast network of shit that only cares about money. My social life is arid, and my friends are about to commit me to a mental facility. I really don't think that merely changing my "attitude" is going to clear any of this up."

"Then why are you here? If you really believe what you just said, then you're wasting time and money here." Larry ambled over to the office door and opened it. "Here you go. Here's your first choice. Walk out of here now and never look back. Just accept what's happening to you without trying to change it. Or, stay here and work through the fear I can see in your eyes. Get rid of it and then access your situation without anything negative clouding your judgement."

I stood up and walked over to where Larry was standing. My eyes were filled with tears as I looked into the hallway. There were two other patients sitting in the waiting area, and they both looked as though their traumas were about to swallow them whole. One was shredding tissues in her hand at an alarming rate, the ribbons of paper falling to the floor as she stared at the wall. The other patient was pacing swiftly back and forth while swinging his arms, and his lips were moving in a rapid rhythm. As I looked at them, I realized that making the wrong decision could land me in the no-man's land they found themselves in, and it looked more terrifying than anything I was worried about.

"Ok, Larry, I trust you." I slowly closed the door and reclaimed my seat, grabbing some tissues as I did so. "Let's exorcise some demons today." Larry sat down in his chair and I began to explain what Linda had told me – maybe he could come up with something that I hadn't. Besides, who else can you trust if not your therapist?

Gossip Mill

My four days of freedom were over, and I dragged myself into the department for my first shift of the week. As I walked down the hall, I noticed a group of therapists talking softly next to the board. One of them turned and saw me, and the group quickly dispersed. I sighed and sat down at a computer terminal to check my email. As I was logging in, Jordan came in and sat on the edge of the desk.

"So, Wonder Woman, I hear you're dating. Where did you dig this one up, the morgue?"

"Why is my social life of so much interest around here? Don't you people have enough to do?" I stood up and walked around Jordan's legs. "And how did you find out?"

"Who else? Alease told me, and everyone else. And the reason we love to hear these things about you is obvious – your sex life is either non-existent or the script for a really bad soap opera. Either way, it's immensely entertaining." Jordan grinned at me, and I felt like slapping his smug face. Alease was the department gossip, and she managed to uncover every juicy detail of the staff's personal lives. Then she proceeded to spread the information to anyone who would listen, and the story would get distorted as it was passed from person to person. Kind of like a sick game of telephone, or a mutating virus.

"Well, Alease should check her sources because she's wrong. I'm not dating anyone at the moment, and if I was I wouldn't tell anyone here. You're all just a bunch of gossiping hags, if you must know." I turned to the coffee machine and poured myself a large cup of black oblivion.

"Oh, I think the lady doth protest too much. You're getting hot sex, aren't you? C'mon, you can tell me." Jordan reached his hand out for my cup, and I slapped it away. "Everyone needs sex, you know. Otherwise you turn into . . . well, take a good look in the mirror." He stood up and faced me. "You know I'm just kidding. But lately you seem more miserable than usual, and it makes me worried. I do care what happens to you, unlike most of the stiffs around here." He put his hand on my shoulder as I tried to turn away. "If you are dating someone, make sure he's not like the two ex-husbands that fucked you over. You deserve better."

"I'm surprised, Jordan. You seem to be displaying human emotions – are you feeling OK?" I reached out and placed the back of my hand on his forehead. "Hmm, you're a little hot."

"Knock it off, asshole. I'm just saying that I want you to be happy. And if you find someone that does it for you, don't run him off." Jordan walked out of the office, and I was left holding my cup and wondering where that spurt of kindness came from.

At that moment, Alease bounced into the office. She was a small, petite woman with bleach-blonde hair that always hung down her back in a ponytail. Her makeup was a shallow imitation of Tammy Faye Baker, and her scrubs were immaculately ironed. Obsessed with appearances, it came as no surprise that there wasn't much to discover beneath the surface. She was a horrible therapist and was constantly making mistakes, but she always managed to charm her way out of any repercussions.

"Alease," I snarled, slowly walking toward her, " I hear that you're very interested in my personal life. Care to name your source?"

"Oh, goodness, I didn't mean to start any trouble," Alease said, lowering her eyes to the table and pretending to straighten a pile of medical journals. "It's been a long time for you and I thought you'd be happy to share the good news." She pulled out a chair and sat down, looking me over with a coy smile. "As for my sources, you know I can't reveal that to you. I would be breaking a confidence, and then what would everyone think?"

"They'd think what I do – that you're a sneaky snake in the grass who shouldn't be trusted with anything." I sat down opposite her and leaned forward over the table.

"Instead of getting into other people's business, why don't you concentrate on something a little more important?"

"And what would that be?"

"Your skills as a therapist. If you spent half the time you spend gossiping on perfecting your techniques, perhaps the rest of us wouldn't have to walk around after you and clean up your messes." I got up from the chair and shoved it back into place. "Is that specific enough for you, or do you need clarification?" She shot me a dirty look, got up from her chair, and started to walk down the hall.

Jordan came back into the office and looked at me sympathetically. "Wow, now you've got her so pissed she's going to tattle on you. Get ready for another write-up, puss."

I walked over to the wall and softly banged my head on it, waiting for the inevitable – Todd's voice calling me into his office.

Danger Zone

"So," Todd said while he put his feet up on his desk, "do you have anything to say for yourself? Or should I just hand the warning to you so that you can refuse to sign it?"

"I'd like for you to explain to me why I am constantly being pulled in here when there are so many other issues that need to be addressed in this department." I was standing by the doorway with my arms folded. Five minutes after Alease walked off Todd had emerged from his cave to invite me for a "chat", and I was more than pissed.

"Really? What issues do you think the department has? And why haven't you come to me with these concerns?" Todd put his feet down and leaned into the desk. "I'll answer that for you. It's because you know YOU are one of the biggest problems we have here. You don't take direction, you are openly hostile to everyone in the building, and your attitude sucks. I have a sneaking suspicion that if you were no longer here, this place would run much more smoothly. Do you have an opinion on that?"

"Yes, I do. I think that you have a personal vendetta against me, and that you would be more than happy to fire my ass right now and throw me out of the hospital for good. So why hasn't that happened yet?" I took a book from off the shelf of dusty journals that Todd had compiled to make him seem intelligent. "See this?" I said, holding up the book. "This is a book written by a person who actually knows what he's talking about. This is a book that I had to read while I was in college training for this position. Have you read this book, Todd, or do you keep it in here to fool the new employees?" I put the book back in its place. "You and I know that I am one of the most experienced therapists here, and that I am also one of the most skilled. The fact that I don't kiss anyone's ass shouldn't matter. I'm here to take care of sick and injured people, not to win a popularity contest."

"I will admit that you can do your job very well, but you have to understand that your personality leaves a lot to be desired." Todd got up and walked over to the shelf, picking up the book that I had just set down. "Books are wonderful, but they don't teach you how to get along with people. And that's something you need to do, or you'll be looking for a new job." He walked over to where I was standing and leaned over me. "I think you know that, as a good manager, I don't allow my personal feelings to interfere with my duties. And since I'm now the ONLY manager in the department, you have no choice but to deal with me."

I could feel my face turning red and my hands clenching into fists. This was never a good sign, and I knew I had to get out of that office before I did something that would have me escorted out of the building by security. I now knew that I would never get any useful information out of Todd, so it would be better to just end this standoff. I unclenched my right hand and held it out to Todd. "OK, I get the picture. Just give me my warning and I'll be on my way. I have to check my assignment and get report."

Todd reached out and grabbed a slip of paper from the desk. Then he walked over to the recycling bin, tore the paper up and dropped it into the bin. He turned to look at me, and his face revealed a sense of swollen triumph.

"That was your warning, but I see I've made my point. I think we'll be getting along just fine now, don't you?" Todd sat back down at the desk and began booting up his laptop. "The warnings will stay in that bin as long as you keep in mind the fact that I am in charge. We may hate each other, but there's a lot of space in this hospital, isn't there?" I turned to leave, relieved that I didn't explode, when he cleared his throat. "And I think Alease deserves an apology. That was some really rough talk, and it's not very professional." As I walked slowly toward the door, I could hear Todd chuckling softly to himself.

Fuck. Now I have to prepare to eat some very chewy crow.

Bad Night

I dragged myself down the hall to the 13th floor, cursing under my breath. I had managed to scrape together a half-hearted apology to Alease before getting my assignment, and she had accepted it with her usual grace. She left the department with a huge smirk on her face, and it was all I could do not to chase her down and shove my stethoscope into her throat. Then I looked at the board and noticed that Todd had split up the work, a task he usually left for the lead therapist to handle. He had given me the busiest piece of work, which was all of the medical floors and the backup emergency room beeper. I was expected to carry three beepers and complete at least 40 treatments in the space of seven hours – a superhuman duty that was normally divided up by two or three therapists. This was a test, and I was either going to pass with flying colors or fail miserably. It was going to be a long night, and I wasn't prepared.

"Oh, hi there, did you get my page?" A nurse was standing at attention by the 13th floor desk, apparently waiting for me to arrive.

"No, but I'm here now. What do you . . . " I was interrupted by the piercing sound of the beeper, which I quickly silenced. The nurse shot me a malignant smile and pointed down the hall.

"I paged you about Room 26. I'm sure you know all about her already, and she's complaining of shortness of breath. Can you go check her out, please? I'll be in the break room if you need anything." The nurse turned and walked back into the room, laughing as she did so. She knew I was in for some trouble, and she seemed relieved to be taken out of the equation for a short time.

Room 26 contained the most angry and disgruntled patient I had ever met. Her name was Mrs. Robertson, and she was an elderly woman that had been stricken with lung cancer after forty years of heavy smoking. She had been suffering from this ailment for six years, and had already had a lobe of her lung removed. She needed oxygen at home just to move around, and she administered nebulizer treatments to herself constantly when she was not hospitalized. She mistakenly seemed to think, as most of my patients did, that these treatments would heal her condition instantly, and demanded them on an hourly basis. Unfortunately, Mrs. Robertson had also acquired a heart condition, and the medications given by a treatment raised her heart rate to an uncomfortable level. I had been told in report that Dr. Hillyer had suspended the hourly treatments as of this shift. If the meds were given on a reasonable time table, there were no problems. But there were no explanations that would convince Mrs. Robertson of these facts, and she constantly threatened to have everyone fired if they did not comply with her exact wishes. This was definitely not what I needed, but I had no choice but to deal with it. I stood outside the door of Room 26, took a cleansing breath, and entered.

"Hello, Mrs. Robertson, I'm from the respiratory department. What can I do for you this evening?" I faced her bed and smiled, hoping that this benign sentence would be the beginning of a civil conversation.

"What do you think I had the nurse page you for? I want my treatment and I want it now." Mrs. Robertson sneered at me, and I noticed that her oxygen was hanging down off the bed.

"Mrs. Robertson, your oxygen is off. Did you forget to wear it when you went to bed?"

"No, I didn't forget to wear it, you stupid moron. That stuff doesn't help me breathe, the treatments do. I don't know why you people even put that shit in here for me. I just need my treatment."

I looked up at the monitor Mrs. Robertson was hooked up to, and noticed that her heart rate was about 150 – very rapid. I reached into my pocket and unfolded my thick sheet of patient assignments. According to my report, Mrs. Robertson had been given a treatment less than two hours ago, and she did not have any more scheduled until the next day. This put me in a tough position.

"I'm concerned about your heart rate, Mrs. Robertson. Let me listen to your lungs and then we can decide . . . "

"Why do I always have to deal with the idiots? I told you, I NEED MY TREATMENT. It doesn't matter what my lungs sound like, and my heart rate has nothing to do with it. Just put the meds on the table and I'll do it myself." Mrs. Robertson sat up in her bed and reached out her hand. I walked over to the monitor and pressed the call button. A pissed-off secretary answered the call.

"What?"

"I need Mrs. Robertson's nurse in here, please. This is respiratory." I tried to keep my voice on an even tone.

"She's on break. Can't you handle this yourself?"

"No, I need her input on this situation. I'm sorry to bother her, but . . . "

"Don't you tell that bitch nurse to come in here," Mrs. Robertson yelled into the speaker. "I don't want her in here. She doesn't know what she's doing any more than this person standing here. Call the nursing supervisor and tell her I have a complaint to make." She leaned back into her pillows, smiling at me. I noticed that she was sweating heavily, and as I looked up at the monitor her pulse rate jumped to 165.

"Mrs. Robertson, I don't think the supervisor needs to be bothered with this. Your heart rate is climbing . . ."

"I don't care!" Mrs. Robertson swung her legs out of the bed and stood up. "None of you people know what I need. Not the doctors, not the nurses, and certainly not you. You don't know what it feels like to be stuck in this bed every day, waiting for something to happen. You have no clue . . ." She stopped speaking and leaned over, panting. Her heart rate was now 180, and it was taking its toll on her overworked body. She grunted and pitched forward, and I managed to catch her before she fell on the hard linoleum floor. I pressed the panic button on her bed and felt for her pulse. It had disappeared, as did any effort to breathe. I quickly turned on the room light and grabbed the rescue bag. As I attached it to the oxygen, the room was suddenly flooded with people.

"What the hell happened in here? I send you in to give her a treatment, and now she's coding? What's wrong with you?" The nurse assigned to Mrs. Robertson had managed to get her fat ass out of the break room in record time, and was standing over me still holding her coffee mug. Now that's professionalism.

"You sent me in here without telling me her heart rate was elevated, and while I was talking to her she collapsed." I growled while pumping breaths with the bag. Four male aides arrived, and together they lifted the limp Mrs. Robertson into her bed and placed a plastic CPR board underneath her body.

"What did you do to make her so upset? This is all your fault, you know." The nurse continued to berate me while idly standing by the bed. She made no move to help in any way, and I was overcome with a sense of disgust.

"Instead of yelling at me, why don't you make yourself useful and go get her chart? The doctors are going to need it when they get here." I moved over to accommodate one aide who had been given the task of cardiac compressions. As he started to pump, I heard the familiar sound of cracking ribs and mentally added a collapsed lung to the list of Mrs. Robertson's problems.

"How dare you talk to me that way? You've got no right. . ." She was cut off by a rush of white-coated interns who ran into the room, eager for some action. Dr. Hillyer quickly followed, and a rush of relief enveloped me.

"Ok, what do we have here? Oh, hello, dear, don't you ever get a day off? I know I don't," Dr. Hillyer gave me a wry smile, and I returned it.

"Where is this patient's chart? Oh my goodness, it's Mrs. Robertson. I just saw her yesterday, was called by the pulmonary doc for a consult." Dr. Hillyer looked at the patient and attempted to find a pulse. "So what was her heart rate before she went down?" He looked expectantly around the room, and Mrs. Robertson's nurse looked down at the floor.

"It was 180, Dr. Hillyer," I replied in a breathless voice. "She was arguing with me about receiving a treatment, and . . ."

"You didn't give it to her, did you?" He asked. I shook my head. "Wonderful. Anyone with half a brain would know not to. So who called you in here?"

"Her nurse." I nodded my head over to where she was standing, and she shot me a hateful look.

"Did you read any of the notes I wrote regarding her orders?" Dr. Hillyer asked. "I specifically stated that these frequent breathing treatments were exacerbating her newly acquired heart condition, and I ordered them to be stopped unless she was extremely short of breath. I also noticed that she was refusing to wear her oxygen, and that any nurse in charge of her care be vigilant about the patient using it." He walked over to where the nurse was standing and looked down at her. "I require an answer, and I require it now."

"Dr. Hillyer, I think we need to intubate her now." I said as I continued to pump breaths into Mrs. Robertson.

"Most definitely." Dr. Hillyer turned to walk out of the room, then changed his mind and stood over Mrs. Robertson's nurse. "I'll deal with you later. You're lucky this therapist was on duty tonight." He strode out of the room to call anesthesia, and moments later the stat call was heard over the intercom system.

The nurse in charge of Mrs. Robertson stood in the doorway, hanging her head with a mournful look. The nursing supervisor rushed into the room and surveyed the situation. She was then almost knocked over by the arrival of the anesthesia team, three doctors with masks tied to their necks and carrying large neon green duffel bags.

"OK, people, Dr. Hillyer said this intubation is urgent. Give me some sedatives and get out of our way." The lead anesthesiologist took the bag from my hand and nodded at me. "You did a great job keeping her airway patent – thanks. Why don't you take a breather and we'll call you when we need to transport her." I stepped away from the bed and walked into the hall. Mrs. Robertson's nurse was flanked on one side by the nursing supervisor and on the other side by Dr. Hillyer. Noone in the group looked pleased, and I didn't want to be involved. I tried to walk past, but Dr. Hillyer grabbed my sleeve and pulled me into the circle.

"This is the person you should be thanking, Wendy," he said while giving me a literal pat on the back. "She always keeps her cool and definitely knows her stuff."

"This person? Really?" Wendy was close friends with Todd, and I'm sure he had given her an earful regarding my recent transgressions. "Well, I have been told some misinformation then. Thank you, dear," she said, "because without you this could have been a much worse situation." She backed away and pulled the nurse in question into the break room to berate her in private. Dr. Hillyer grinned at me.

"What was that all about?"

"Well," I said, looking down, "I've been having some problems lately, and . . . "

"Problems? Oh, I know what you mean. You don't kowtow like they want around here." Dr. Hillyer leaned over and began speaking in a low tone. "I had exactly the same problem when I was a lowly CNA. Everyone told me I had a huge attitude problem and that I would never get far. But look at me now." He straightened up and rubbed his hands together. "Don't let anyone tell you that you're not good at what you do. So what if you don't fit in? Stay just the way you are, and if you have any more problems I will be more than happy to vouch for you." He turned and watched as the three anesthesiologists walked out of Mrs. Robertson's room and gave him a thumbs-up.

"Let's go check on our patient, shall we?" Dr. Hillyer held out his arm, and I took it with a grin. Together we strolled into the room, while everyone in the hallway looked at us in shock.

Much later, after I transferred Mrs. Robertson to the ICU, I sat down at an unattended computer terminal to chart everything that had just occurred. Suddenly, a mug of hot coffee was shoved into my face. I looked up and smiled as I saw Jordan grinning back at me.

"Thought you could use this after all the hullabaloo. So what's on the menu next? Going up to the helipad and attempting to fly?"

"Jealous? I know that your only reason for having this job is to deal with all the codes and traumas."

Jordan assumed an injured look and sat down next to me. "Well, I've never been so insulted. But actually you've got it wrong. The only reason I keep this job is for the paycheck." He looked around to make sure no one else could hear him and then leaned in close to me. "I've been meaning to tell you that I'm about to leave this stinking cesspool. I found a job elsewhere and tomorrow I'm marching into Amy's office to give my two weeks' notice. I wanted to tell you before the rumor mill got hold of it."

"Where are you going?" I asked without trying to betray my sense of disappointment.

"I'm going to be selling ventilators to hospitals. Isn't that a hoot? Me in a suit – it's hilarious." Jordan shifted in his seat and looked down at the floor before continuing. "I mean, I love the action around here and working with patients really fulfills me. But this place isn't about that anymore – it's all about the money. Everyone's worried about the cuts Medicare has instituted, and so the higher-ups are investing all their money into how this place looks. They want to fool the patients into believing that our hospital is the best just because we have marble floors in the lobby. Then once they get in here, they keep them for as long as they can to get the most amount of money and then boot them out regardless of where they end up. It's shameful, and I can't do it anymore."

"Kinda like presenting yourself as an exotic dancer when you're really a stripper. I get what you're saying, Jordan. If the management were more honest I would respect them more. But then the patients would go elsewhere, so it's a Catch-22."

Jordan took a slip of paper out of his pocket and handed it to me. "I told them all about you, and they want to hire you too. We could sell as a team – imagine that. C'mon, you know you hate this place as much as I do. Come with me. It's a guaranteed offer to make three times the money you make now, and you can make your own hours." I looked at the paper while Jordan stood and watched me. "I understand you have patient care at the top of your list of priorities, but it's not possible to do that here. Just think about how good it would feel to walk into Todd's office in the morning and tell him to fuck off."

I smiled and handed the paper back to him. "I'm not a salesperson, Jordan, I'm a caretaker. I like taking care of people who need help. How will I accomplish that selling equipment? I might as well quit my job here and sell cars. Please don't take this wrong – I really appreciate the offer and it sounds tempting. But I wouldn't be satisfied with that kind of life. Maybe I'm naïve, but I think I make a difference here and that gives me a purpose. Can you understand?"

Jordan sighed and stood up. "Somehow I knew that would be your answer. But you can't blame me, can you?" He patted the top of my head. "Poor, silly idealist. I'm going to miss you, asshead. If you ever change your mind, just call me and it's a done deal."

I watched him walk away and wondered if I should have told Jordan about my conversation with Linda. What would he say if he knew about all the subterfuge that was going on around here? As these thoughts were running through my head, I noticed Wendy walking with a man and woman in street clothes. The woman was crying, and the man had his head down while rubbing the woman's back. Wendy noticed where I was sitting, said something in the woman's ear, and walked over to me.

"I'm glad you're still here. Those people are Mrs. Robertson's relatives – her daughter and son-in-law. They came in when they heard what happened, and they're going to see her now." She motioned to the woman, who walked slowly over to the desk.

"Mrs. Nander, this is the therapist I was telling you about," Wendy said while pointing at me. The grieving woman looked at me for a moment and then leaned over to give me a heartfelt hug. A few of her tears wet the shoulder of my scrub top, and I felt both overwhelmed and embarrassed.

"My mother has been so difficult to deal with ever since she got diagnosed with cancer," Mrs. Nander said while dabbing at her eyes with a tissue. "She lives with us, and we had a hard time even getting her to wear her oxygen. We found out two days ago that she's still smoking – SMOKING. Can you believe that?" I nodded my head sympathetically. "I want to thank you for standing up to her and doing the right thing. Sometimes I think she's so obstinate because she misses my dad so much. Maybe she wants to die so she can be with him again. Whatever the reasons, her attitude is awful and I can't imagine what you guys have to do just to take care of her." She put her hand on my shoulder. "You should be proud of yourself for the work you do, and I'm sure your parents are proud too."

I ducked my head to suppress the tears forming in my eyes. Of course this woman had no idea that my parents weren't around anymore, but it was still a sore subject for me. I composed myself and stood up to shake Mrs. Nander's hand. "Thank you for saying all that. You have no idea how much it means to me."

"Why don't you come with us to see my mother? We were just on our way there." Mrs. Nander motioned to the closed door of the ICU, and I shook my head.

"I'd love to , but duty calls." I swept my hand over the three beepers hanging from my shirt. "There are people waiting for me, but I'll come check on her later if you like." I picked up my assignment sheets lying on the desk and shoved them into my pocket. "We have an excellent therapist in the ICU that will take good care of your mom, and Dr. Hillyer is in there now monitoring the situation. She's in good hands, and I'm sure she's comfortable. I'm sorry I can't continue this conversation, but I have work to do and I'm sure you're anxious to see your mother. I'll see you later." I shook Mrs. Nander's hand and walked down the hall while Wendy looked on approvingly.

As I pressed the elevator button, I looked out the window of the 13th floor. The city seemed quiet, and the sky was full of twinkling stars. The moon was full and luminous, and its reflected light hurt my eyes. Then I heard the staccato whine of an ambulance on the street speeding its way to the ER, and my beepers began screaming in tune with the siren. My spell broken, I abandoned the elevator and ran toward the stairwell.

Hemorrhage

As I parked my car in the apartment lot, I thought about all the events of the night before. I had run down to the ER to find three gunshot victims that had been at the same house partying. Apparently drugs were involved, and there had been a drive-by shooting at the residence. One of the patients had not arrived by ambulance, but had been driven to the ER entrance and dumped unceremoniously onto the sidewalk. The driver had not stuck around, screeching off the moment the patient had hit the cement. This was not a common occurrence, but it wasn't the first time I'd seen it happen either. I helped the ER therapist stabilize all three patients while the other therapists on duty took my original assignment from me and completed the treatments. The last two hours of my shift had been spent in the MRI department, and I had been grateful for the break in the action. By the time I had been relieved of my work, it was past punch-out time. I didn't have time to check on Mrs. Robertson, but I intended to do so tonight when I came in.

I trudged toward my building after driving home when my phone began to vibrate. I looked at the caller ID and noticed Sid's number. Smiling, I answered.

"Hey there, beautiful. I wanted to catch you before you fell asleep. How was your night?" Sid inhaled deeply into the receiver, and I knew he was lighting up a cigarette.

"Oh, it was just dandy. Peachy. Best day I've ever had in the seventh circle of Hell." I quipped as I unlocked my apartment door. I threw my work bag on the kitchen counter and opened the refrigerator. Damn, I hadn't had time to go shopping and there was practically nothing to drink. I poured a glass of iced coffee even though I had to sleep, and starting stripping off my scrubs.

"How was your day? Did you get any further on the recording?" Sid was working on a new album and had just started rehearsing with a band he had put together.

"You mean yesterday? About as good as your night. The fucking guitarist developed an attitude to match his enormous ego and quit. Now I'm going to have to do that part of the track myself. Pain in the ass, but I can do it. Listen to me whine – that must sound like such crap after everything you have to put up with."

I walked into the bedroom and put on my favorite pajamas, gray with silver hearts. I peeled back my comforter and crawled into bed, juggling the phone at my ear. "Nope. Everyone has shit they have to put up with. Why should my problems be any more important than yours?"

"I know you don't think you're special, but you are. You have a job taking care of other people and you have to put up with the manager from Hell. You do so many good things for so many people. Believe me when I say that most people would never be able to get through one day of being you without becoming a drug addict or going nuts."

I smiled into the phone. "Thank you for all the compliments, but I'm no one special. Anyone could do what I do."

"I don't think so. I couldn't do it. And you haven't had the easiest life, either. Your parents gone, those asshole ex-husbands . . . I admire you."

I could feel myself blushing and burrowed deeper under the covers. "Enough with the mutual admiration society. I have to go to sleep so I'm going to hang up."

"You want me to come over and sing you a lullaby?" I heard him chuckle under his breath.

"Very funny. Good night."

"Have a good sleep."

I hung up and plugged my phone into the charger. I pressed my face into the pillow and smiled. Sid had been calling me every morning after my shift, propping me up and making me feel better. I noticed that I slept better after his call, and that I had a little spring in my step that had never been there before. Things were looking up on the social front – I just wished that work wasn't such a bitch.

Just then my phone began to vibrate. I was tempted to ignore it, but I sat up and looked at the caller ID. It was Thia, and I knew she would continue to press redial until I picked up. Sighing, I put the phone to my ear.

"Thia, what a surprise. You know what time it is?"

"Yeah, this is when normal people wake up and go to work. When are you going to get your shift changed and stop living like a vampire?"

"Why aren't you at work? Have you quit your job so you can nag me fulltime?" I shifted in the bed and grabbed the TV remote.

"I don't have to be there until 10 today. My hours got cut because of the NEW MINIMUM WAGE. You know, the usual shit. Anyway, I'm calling to see if you thought about our conversation the other night. Have you seen a doctor about that physical?"

"You know how I feel about doctors, Thia. Most of them are useless and just want to use you to get a fatter fee with lab tests. There's nothing wrong with me."

"Oh really? What about the fact that you've lost about twenty pounds in three months? What about your hair falling out? The trouble sleeping?"

"There are all good explanations for that. I've had trouble sleeping ever since my parents died. I've lost weight because I eat less on the night shift."

"And the hair? What about that? Don't tell me you have a bullshit explanation for that. Noone at your age loses their hair for no reason."

"Thia, please. I have a nasty headache and I have to go back to the hospital tonight. Can't we talk about this some other time?"

"Listen to me , you stubborn mule. If you don't talk to me about this right now, I'm going to drive over there and drag your ass out." Thia's voice had an edge to it, and I knew that there was not going to be any negotiation.

"All right, all right. I'll talk to you about it. What would you like me to say?"

"I'd like you to tell me you have a doctor's appointment or a job interview. Either way it would improve your health. Doesn't Sid have anything to say about this?"

"Sid appreciates the way I feel about the medical establishment. He doesn't think there's anything going on that a vacation wouldn't fix."

"OK, so why did he just text me and tell me he's worried about you?"

"How is it that he has your number? And why would he text you? Why wouldn't he just tell me? I just got off the phone with him."

"He knows how much trouble men have given you over the years and he doesn't want you to push him away. He has a point."

I shifted in my bed and sighed. "We've been dating for a little while and he seems like a decent person. But he shouldn't worry about me and neither should you. I can take care of myself."

"You're doing a bang-up job. You look like a survivor from a zombie apocalypse. And you've got a great guy dangling on your hook that you refuse to reel in. I can't wrap my head around your personal choices."

"Well, then I'll explain them to you," I snapped, getting out of bed and pacing beside my bedroom window. "I don't want to see a doctor because I don't want to know if something's wrong with me. I work in a hospital, remember? I see what happens to helpless patients every day, and I'd rather be run over by a truck than deal with that. And as far as Sid is concerned, I don't want him getting too close to me because he'll get an itch the minute I feel safe with him. I can't handle another relationship blowing up in my face and I'd rather be alone. Do you understand that? Is that enough for you, or do you need more?" By this time I was yelling into the phone, and I could hear my anger reflected off the walls.

There was a long pause, and then Thia clucked through her teeth. "Shit, dude. That was harsh and unnecessary. If you wanted to be left alone so badly, all you had to do was say so. I'll be seeing you around." There was a silence, and then a click. Fuck.

I put the phone down and laid my head heavily onto the pillows. Thia was right – that was harsh. All she wanted to do was make sure I was OK, and I overreacted. She had been my friend for years and had stuck by me through the most unimaginable situations. Why had I turned on her now? I was going to have to concoct the most contrite apology the world had ever seen, and it had to be fast. As I was thinking of what to say, my phone began vibrating again. I looked at the caller ID – Hannah. I put the phone back down – apparently word travels fast. Let her leave a message – I had to sleep on this.

Last Chance

I swam up from a deep sleep to hear loud banging on my front door. I looked at my clock by the bed – 3:45 pm. I put my head under my pillow and closed my eyes, hoping the sound would fade away to nothing.

Bang, bang, bang.

Bang, bang, bang.

BANG.

Cursing under my breath, I got up and staggered to the door.

"Someone better be dead or close to it," I yelled as I looked through the peephole. It was Sid, and he didn't look happy. I undid the bolt and swung the door open.

"What the fuck! I've been pounding on that door for fifteen minutes now. What's wrong with you?" Sid stepped over the threshold and leaned against the kitchen counter.

"What's wrong is that I was sleeping, you ass. What is so important that it can't wait until I'm awake?" I was aware of standing in front of him in just my pajamas, but at this point I didn't care.

"Thia called me a little while ago and told me you'd gone off the deep end. You yelled at her over the phone and was telling her some bullshit about not trusting me. Is that true? I thought we were past that."

I sighed and sat down on the counter. "I'm sorry that you got dragged into this drama, but it happens from time to time with me and Thia. She has no boundaries and seems to think of me as her surrogate daughter. But not to worry, I'm fine."

Sid walked over to where I was sitting and took both of my hands in his. "You didn't answer my question."

"I don't know how to answer it. I want to trust you, I really do, but I don't think I could handle it if you got tired of me and cheated. That's what always seems to happen, and

I'm sick of it." I tried to pull my hands away but he held them fast and looked into my eyes.

"If you don't take a chance you'll never know what could have happened, good or bad. I have never cheated on anyone, it's always been the other way around. So I know where you're coming from, and I have the same fears. Who's to say that you won't get tired of me? I'm no prize, believe me."

I closed my eyes as I squeezed his hands. When would this mistrust end? I felt a deep surge of warmth within me as I pondered this question. It seemed that the decision had been made.

"You know what? You're right. I want to take a chance , and you're the only person I would take it with," I said and eased myself off the counter. I moved closer to him and took his face in my hands. "I feel safe with you, and I've been denying that to myself out of fear. But now it's time to accept it." I gently pulled his face to mine and sought out his lips.

This kiss was unlike any I'd ever felt before. Soft and yielding, it also had the force of urgency. We kissed and held each other, finding what we both had been missing for so long. I felt his tongue part my lips and gently explore the inner regions of my mouth. My tongue traced circles around his lip ring, faster and faster until it was moving at a frenzied pace.

I felt Sid's hands slip under my clothes and did nothing to stop him. They traveled at a lazy pace back and forth across my back, then moved downward. I moved my hands up and tangled my fingers in his hair, making knots in the tendrils.

He pulled away and looked at me. "Should we move this discussion into your bedroom?"

I took his hand and tugged. "Yep. Judging from that kiss, I can tell we have a lot to talk about." I led him into the bedroom and grabbed my phone.

"What are you doing? You don't have anything to gossip about yet," Sid said as he sat down on the bed and tried to pull me closer. I put the phone to my ear and held up my finger to stop him from talking.

"Yeah, hi Lenny, you know who. No, no . . . look, don't pull that shit with me. I'm perfectly aware of the eight-hour limit for calling in, and I'm getting the call in just under the wire. I'm not scheduled until 11, and I know Sandra's been looking for OT so just call her OK? I'm feeling like I should spend some time in bed." I hung up and put the phone down on the bedside table.

Sid looked up at me expectantly, with a longing in his eyes I'd never seen with anyone I'd been with before.

"So . . . what should we talk about now?"

I stripped off my clothes and stood before him, allowing my hair to spread down across my back. "Do you see anything that might spark a conversation?"

"Nope. Guess we'll have to find something else to do," Sid said and took off his shirt. He threw it on the other side of the room and grabbed my hand.

The night I spent with Sid was the most memorable one I'd ever had with a man. He was slow and sweet, easing me into the moment with gentle movements. As the evening progressed, I threw abandon to the wind and let myself go completely. I was rewarded with so many orgasms my muscles were sore. Not that I was complaining, and neither was Sid.

After it was over, we held each other and talked softly of our lives to each other – things we'd both kept secret from the rest of the world for years. I fell asleep in his arms, comforted by the presence of another person in my slumber.

When I woke up the following morning, I opened my eyes and found myself alone. The familiar feeling of dread enveloped me until I saw a fresh iced coffee sitting next to my phone, with a note propped on it.

"Had to go to an early rehearsal. If I'd known what was going to happen I would have cancelled it. Didn't want to wake you. Don't worry – I'll come back tonight. And tomorrow. And the next day. Sid."

I held the note to my chest and smiled, satisfied that I hadn't been left holding the bag, so to speak. I put the note down and grabbed the coffee, sipping it from the straw. Strong, with lots of cream and one sugar – perfect. Just like last night had been. For a moment everything seemed perfect, and I sat back on the pillows, wanting to relish every second of this bliss.

Just then my phone rang. I picked it up, hoping it was Sid, but the caller ID said Hannah . Sighing, I looked at the clock – ten fifteen. I lifted the phone.

Caregiver Overload

I had floated through the rest of the day, not caring about sleep. After I talked to Hannah, I called Thia and apologized – it was an Oscar-winning performance. I cleaned the apartment and did all my laundry, rejoicing when I found Sid's shirt in with the dirty clothes. I pressed it to my face and smelled his odor before dropping it into the washer drum. I found myself smiling at everyone and blushing when I thought about my night with Sid. Nothing could ruin my mood – well, nothing but going to work.

As I locked my car and wandered toward the elevator, I wondered whether tonight would be a change of pace just as my personal life had taken a swerve toward happiness. I walked past the ER entrance and noticed a large number of police cars in all the parking spaces. There were usually at least two or three cop cars there at any given time, but tonight five local police and two state troopers were there. This was unusual, but I chalked it up to possible gang activity and walked into the hospital lobby.

"Hey!" A burly security guard accosted me as I was about to get onto the elevator. "I need to see your ID badge pronto, missy."

"Since when do we check badges at this time of night? Is this another new policy?" I reached in my pocket and pulled out my badge. The guard took it and looked it over suspiciously.

"There's a situation upstairs and we need to monitor everybody. Here you go," he said, handing the badge back to me, "sorry for any inconvenience."

"So can you tell me what's going on?" I said, moving a little closer to the guard. "Am I in danger?"

The guard looked around to make sure no one was watching us, and then leaned down. "There's a former employee up on the helipad threatening to jump. I have no idea how he got up there, but there's been a standoff and he's refusing to get down. As a matter of fact, he used to work in your department."

A cold chill took hold of my neck and froze my spine. "Do you happen to know his name?" I asked.

"Tom something, I think. Man, he's nuts. I'm glad I won't be the one cleaning up the sidewalk after he takes a dive." The guard chuckled and then glanced at my angry face. "Hey, sorry. Are you a friend of his or something?"

"Something like that, asshole. You should work on your people skills because they suck." I pushed past him and ran into the nearest elevator.

By the time I reached the department, the atmosphere was thick with tension. Amy and Todd were in the hallway, speaking to several therapists who were gathered in the hallway. Amy saw me run in and rapidly walked over to me.

"I'm sure you've heard the bad news. Tom got access to the helipad with his old ID badge about two hours ago. He's barricaded himself in one corner and says he's going to jump. I have no idea what we're going to do." Amy was sweating, something I'd never seen her do. Todd joined our group and gave me a brief nod, then whispered something into Amy's ear.

"Excuse me," she said, and hurried away with a waiting police officer. Todd looked me over and gave me a smirk.

"Sure hope you don't end up like Tom," he said while scrutinizing his cell phone. "It seems he just couldn't stand not working here. Now he's going to be taken to the loony bin for a long time – if he doesn't jump, that is."

"You are one of the most despicable human beings I have ever met, and you should be ashamed of yourself," I snarled into Todd's face. "How can you find humor in this situation? Don't you have any decency whatsoever?"

"Decency? Is that what you're calling it? I call it weakness," Todd said. "The man loses his job and six weeks later he decides to climb a roof and threatens to end it all. What a pathetic piece of shit. There's dozens of hospitals in the area, so why couldn't he find another job? No, instead of doing that he drowns in his own self-pity."

I looked at Todd's smug face and suddenly a horrible thought popped into my head. "You blackballed him, didn't you?" Todd's face caved in, and for a moment I saw his panic at my revelation. "You're the one who recommended to Amy that he be fired, and then you called all of your buddies who work in other places and discreetly talked shit about Tom. You made sure that he would never get another job in this field."

"You have no proof of that." Todd's face turned red, and he took my arm to lead me further down the hall where no one would be able to hear us talking.

"Spoken like a guilty man. Why would you do something like that? What possible reason would you have to ruin Tom's life?" I yanked my arm out of his grip and planted both feet firmly on the floor, waiting for an answer.

Todd looked down at the floor. "I have no idea what you're talking about."

"Gutless," I whispered under my breath.

Todd grabbed the collar of my scrub shirt and pulled me back. "What did you say?"

"Get your hands off me," I yelled, pulling away from him. A few people in the hallway turned to see what was happening, and Todd quickly escorted me into his office. He slammed the door shut and stood against it.

"I want to know what you called me back there," he said.

"I think you heard me loud and clear, but I'll go ahead and repeat it. I said you're gutless," I spat out.

" I could fire you right now just for that comment," Todd said, moving away from the door and positioning himself one inch from my face. "I thought we had an understanding."

I looked up and moved closer to him. "I thought we did too, but I had no idea what a fucked person you are. It's true, isn't it? You got rid of Tom just as easily as you would scrape dogshit off the bottom of your shoe. There's no one here to listen to us talking – you're safe."

Todd sighed and put his hands on my shoulders. "I'm not telling you shit. I'm in charge, remember? And even if I did admit to 'plotting' against Tom, who would believe you?"

I shook his hands off and backed away. "You're right, Todd. Noone would ever believe that you would deliberately target a therapist. But I mistakenly thought that you were a man – that is, a person that would stand behind his actions. I guess I was wrong." I walked around him and opened the office door.

"Where you do think you're going?" Todd said.

"I'm going up to the helipad," I said. "I want Tom's side of the story, since you won't give me yours."

"You're not allowed up there," Todd yelled, following me down the hallway. "There's security, cops . . . you'll never get anywhere near him."

"Watch me," I said softly. "Why do you care? He's a nut, right? Noone will believe him, either. So what's the harm in two losers like me and Tom engaging in a little small talk about what a fucknut you are?" I smiled, and a sense of calm I hadn't felt in several years settled over me and came to rest in my stomach. I turned and jogged toward the elevators.

The helipad was, obviously, on the roof of the hospital. There was one elevator dedicated to its access, and a key was needed to operate it. However, those of us who worked here knew of another way to get up to it. A hidden flight of stairs that started on the 13th floor led directly up to the dispatcher room on the top floor, and this room was next to the helipad. Some therapists liked to hang out in the radio room and wait for calls to come in, others would sleep on the cot there to hide from the supervisors. I had never utilized this hideaway, but I knew of its existence. I got off the elevator on the 13th floor and located the door marked "Utility". It opened with no resistance, and I began climbing the stairs.

I reached the top floor and cautiously cracked the door open an inch. I peeked out and saw that no one was near the door. Radio crackles and shouting floated through the air, and I saw several people standing near the helipad entrance. I crept through the door and walked slowly through the dispatcher room. There was no one manning the desk, and I thought the dispatcher must have been removed as a precaution.

I moved through the radio room and approached the helipad. I saw Amy standing with several state troopers, wiping her eyes with a tissue. One of the troopers was patting her back, and another one was taking notes on a small pad. There were several nursing supervisors gathered in a corner talking, and I spotted a man in a suit speaking rapidly into his phone. The scene was chaotic, and amazingly no one appeared to be guarding the door leading to the helipad. I slipped quietly through the crowd, avoiding Amy, and crept through the door.

The helipad was lit on several sides by floodlights, and the surface shone slickly with falling rain. There was a group of uniformed men and women standing on the right side of the roof, conversing quietly. No other sound emanated from the area, and the effect was one of eerie foreshadowing. I looked to the left and saw a small figure sitting in the corner with his head in his hands. Tom.

"Hey," I said, and Tom looked up. "I came up when I heard you were here. Don't you have anywhere else to hang out?"

"No, no, no . . ." one of the security officers shouted when he heard my voice. "I don't know how you got up here, but you need to leave immediately." He sprinted over to where I was standing and grabbed my arm. He started to haul me away when a piercing cry caught his attention.

"Let her go, or I'll jump right now," Tom said, standing up. He propped himself up on the wall and looked down at the road. "I see news cameras down there, and I think they'll be able to get a great shot of me plunging to my death. Do you want that?" The guard shook his head and released his grip.

"You can come over here, hon. You're the only one I want to talk to, anyway," Tom said. I started walking slowly over to the corner.

Suddenly Amy burst through the entrance door. "Wait . . ." she screamed, "what are you doing up here? You're only going to make things worse . . ."

"How is that possible, Amy?" Tom said. "You're the reason I'm up here. You and Todd. So if anyone needs to leave, it's you."

"Me? You're blaming me for this?" Amy said. "I can't wait to hear this explanation."

"You agreed to fire me, Amy! How could you do that after all the years I've worked here?"

"There were several good reasons that were brought to my attention . . ."

"By Todd, right?" Tom shouted. Amy looked down. "Yep, Todd. The man that I was going to replace. Except at the last minute, he 'uncovered' evidence that I was faking treatments. All of a sudden, I was seen as a criminal. A bad therapist and a bad caretaker. And I was fired." Tom paced to the other side of the helipad. "Did you ever question the evidence that Todd brought to you? Did you ask him to produce something more than the sheets he'd printed himself?"

I looked over at Amy in shock. "Is that why Tom was fired?" Because of one person's statement?" Amy was still looking down, tears falling to the ground. I swiftly walked over to her and grabbed her shoulders, forcing her to look into my face. "I asked you a question, Amy."

"He had all the sheets. I had no idea he was lying," Amy sobbed. "I've been so busy with all the extra duties I've been given lately that I was depending on Todd to run the department. He seemed so dependable, I never questioned his skills. But then therapists started coming into my office and complaining that he was unorganized and unfair."

"Did you listen?" I said while keeping an eye on Tom, who was again pacing back and forth across the helipad.

"I didn't want to listen at first. I just wanted to think that everyone was tense because of the workload. Everyone complains when there's more work to do," Amy said, pausing to blow her nose.

"Look, ladies, we have a situation here," one of the state troopers said while patting Amy's back. "All of this talk isn't going to resolve our crisis."

"I disagree," I snarled. "I think the only reason Tom's up here is to get some attention called to him. He's not crazy, he just wants to be heard. He wants to be redeemed. So, Amy," I said while turning to face her, "what's the rest of the story?"

"After the tenth therapist came in to complain, I decided to talk to Todd," Amy said. "He became very defensive and accused the therapists of sabotage. It was then that I spoke to Tom about taking Todd's place. He is such a good therapist, and I thought he would make a wonderful manager. A week later, Todd came into my office and showed me the sheets he'd 'uncovered'."

"And then you fired me," Tom yelled from the helipad, his hands forming loose fists at his sides. "You didn't even investigate the possibility that the assignment sheets were fake. You never questioned Todd's integrity, even though everyone else did."

"Why the hell do you think I talked to you about replacing him?" Amy screamed back. "I wanted a manager that everyone would be able to depend on and respect. Obviously Todd wasn't that person, but I couldn't very well fire him when he had evidence that you were charting treatments you had not given. How would that look?"

"To whom? Who were you worried about? The higher-ups? I think they would be way more concerned about a member of management faking evidence to have their competition fired." Tom stopped pacing and stood at the edge of the helipad. "After I left here, I couldn't find another job. Todd made sure, without being obvious, that the story got around to all of his respiratory cronies. I didn't know what was going on until a friend at a homecare company admitted it to me. It wasn't enough that he got rid of me – he had to make sure I never worked as a therapist again."

"I am so sorry," Amy said, and started to walk toward the platform.

"Stop right there," Tom cried. "I don't trust you, Amy. Who knows what the suits have been telling you while I've been up here? I know the only thing they care about is the negative publicity I'm garnering."

"Do you trust me, Tom?" I said while slowly walking back onto the helipad. "I'm on your side here. I was heartbroken when I heard you were fired, and so was most of the department. I'll be your advocate – but only if you stop putting yourself in danger." I stopped walking and held out my arms. "If you don't get down from here, something tragic is going to happen. It's not worth it, is it?"

The helipad became eerily quiet as everyone held their breath, waiting for Tom's decision. I froze, not daring to move closer. The only sounds I heard were Amy's ragged sobs and the security radios, both producing distracting static. Tom looked up at the sky, trying to find the answer in the clouds circling overhead. He threw up his hands, and then he looked at me.

"C'mon, Tom," I said, still holding out my arms. Tom hesitated and then ran straight into my embrace.

"Make sure no one shoots me, OK?" he whispered into my ear.

Tom and I walked together arm in arm toward the radio room when we were stopped in our tracks by a tall man in an immaculate dark suit. His face was red, and he was obviously displeased with the situation. He looked vaguely familiar, but I couldn't place where I had seen him before.

"You're not getting off that easy," he said, grabbing Tom's arm and attempting to haul him away. I broke his grip on Tom and stood in front of him.

"Who are you? Why do you want to make this any worse than it already is?" I said, planting both feet firmly on the ground.

"You, young lady, have no idea who you're talking to. I'm the CEO of this hospital, and I was woken out of a sound sleep to dash over here because this delinquent had come up to the roof and was threatening to jump."

"Oh, I'm so sorry someone interrupted your beauty sleep. I guess the only reason you show your face is when your cash cow is in danger of not filling your wallet up fast enough." I shoved my finger into his chest. "I know you're terrified of negative press, Mr. Letiper. But what is the press going to say about this man's story? A good and intelligent medical worker fired for false evidence that no one bothered to authenticate – and he was fired by a man who knew he was going to be replaced. I think that sounds like a very juicy headline for any newscaster, don't you?"

"You wouldn't dare," Mr. Letiper breathed while attempting to walk past me. "That would be breaking the confidentiality agreement you signed when you were hired. Are you willing to give up your job for this loser?"

A deep sense of calm rushed through my lungs, filling them with a crystalline sense of purpose. I smiled and looked up at the sky, which amazingly had cleared itself of clouds in a split second. A full moon beamed down, filling the air with golden rays of reflected sunlight. The crowd of people assembled on the rooftop took no notice, but I knew a sign when it smacked me in the face and I wasn't going to ignore it.

"Yes, I am, Mr. Letiper. You can take this job and shove it straight up your ass," I said with a twisted smirk. Tom tugged at my sleeve and shook his head.

"Please don't do this. Don't ruin your life just for me."

"I'm not. I think for the first time in a very long time, I'm doing the right thing. And as for your job, I'm pretty sure any labor attorney in the state would love to sink their teeth into this case. You'll probably end up being the boss after all." I stepped back a few feet and inhaled deeply.

"Tom, I want to say how sorry I am again for all of this happening," Amy said. "I would like to speak with you and try to get this settled. Mr. Letiper, are you in favor of that?"

Mr. Letiper looked at Amy, then at me. "Do you think we could keep this incident out of the limelight, so to speak?" He offered me his hand. "I had no idea that this man had been victimized in the way you described. You may not believe me, but I do care about more than money and negative press. I will personally see to it that this gentleman's name is cleared. Is that a deal?"

I looked at his hand and shook my head. "Mr. Letiper, you'll have to speak to my colleague about that. I promise I won't mention anything to the press about what happened up here, but that doesn't mean the situation is resolved. We have a lot of problems in our department that need to be addressed. If you really mean what you say and you care about your employees, you'll take this opportunity to investigate what goes on in your building when you're not here."

I put my hand on Tom's shoulder. "I guess I've caused enough trouble for one night, Tom. I'm glad you're going to get some justice. I'll just be going home . . . "

Amy moved to stand in my path. "Now you don't actually think you're going anywhere, do you? I can't accept your resignation, and I don't think Mr. Letiper will either. You are one of our best therapists, and I can't let you go."

I smiled and took my cell phone out of my pocket. "I'm sorry to put it this way, Amy, but you should have thought about that before any of this happened. Until changes are made, I can't put myself through this hell anymore. You have my number, but don't wait too long. I've suddenly realized that I have options I never knew existed, and I might take one of them." I walked past Amy and through the crowd that had gathered at the edge of the helipad and put the phone to my ear.

"Sid? I knew you'd be awake. Meet me at my house . . . and bring a bottle of champagne. We've got some celebrating to do."

Clear . . .

I open my eyes to the sunlight streaming through the windows. It floats through the cracks in my blinds, filling the air with liquid fire. I stretch luxuriously, raising my arms above my head and knocking the covers off my shoulders.

"Hey . . . " a muffled voice trickles from the other side of the bed. "What are you doing up so early? Are you insane?"

"No, just happy and excited to get to work. Never thought you'd hear me say that, did you?" I grin at Sid as he rubs his eyes and sits up.

"No, I have to admit that. But it's a lovely sight to see and hear . . . just like you." He wraps his arms around me and gently pulls me back down onto the mattress. "You don't have to get up right this second, do you?"

"Nope. I have a whole hour." I snuggle up on his chest, feeling the strength of his arms on my back. "And I can't think of a better way to spend it."

Two hours later, I am dressed in my scrubs and driving my car to the hospital. I swing into the parking garage and park on the second floor near the elevator. As I walk to the stairs I smile and wave at everyone I see – and the reactions I get range from complete ignorance to cheery salutations. I practically skip down the sidewalk and into the hospital, pausing long enough to grab an iced coffee from the café in the lobby. It's filled with people from the morning rush, and I struggle to get to the cream dispenser.

"Hey, don't fill up on caffeine yet. There's plenty to go around in the conference room," a voice says behind me, and I turn to see Tom standing next to the sugar packets.

"Well, you know a vampire like me can use all the coffee she can get at this time of the day. I'm not used to seeing sunlight and crowds of people. It's almost as if I'm . . . normal."

"Let's not get ahead of ourselves," Tom chuckles. He puts his arm around my shoulder and steers me toward the elevators. "You ready for today?"

"As ready as I'm ever going to be, I guess." I push the up button and look up at him. "Do you actually think I have anything to offer these people?"

"If I didn't, you wouldn't be here. Now have some confidence in yourself – you're going to be wonderful." Tom stepped into the waiting elevator and held the door for me. A crowd of visitors followed us in, and I pressed the button for 5. We stood in silence until the doors opened and deposited us on the fifth floor. I took a deep breath as Tom and I walked down the hall and into a large room. Several young and expectant faces turned toward us, and we took our place at the front of the room.

"Ok, everybody, I hope you're ready for a long and grueling day of learning. This is your first clinical day, and I'm sure you're all nervous but there's no reason to be. Today is your beginning of a rewarding career caring for others who need your help, and you should all be very proud of the choice you've made to be here." Tom paused to clear his throat and then gestured toward me. "Let me introduce you to your new clinical instructor. She's a very experienced therapist with years of practice under her belt, but she has a much more important qualification. This person knows more about empathy and caring than anyone I've ever worked with, and I hope she'll be able to pass those qualities to you. So, without further delay, I'll turn the floor over to her."

Tom winked at me and walked to the back of the room.

I took my place and stood behind the podium, looking around the room. So many students, all eager to learn and grow in their knowledge. Not one of them knew what they were getting themselves into, and I almost felt sorry for them.

Almost.

"That was the most awesome thing I've ever seen. And on my first day, too!"

I followed the young man out into the hall of the emergency department and chuckled. I had brought the students down here when I heard that a multi-car accident was coming in, and the learning experience had been very valuable. One of the victims of the accident had been ejected from the car and through the windshield, and his injuries had been so severe that a surgeon had been forced to perform some impromptu repairs in the trauma room before transporting him to the OR. The students had been transfixed as they watched from the observation area, and some had been scribbling furiously in their notebooks.

The ten students gathered around a table in the lobby and waited anxiously for me as I joined them. Their faces betrayed their excitement, and also their fatigue.

"OK guys, I think that's enough for one day, don't you? Why don't you take off from here and I'll see you on Wednesday."

A small slight girl with her hair in a severe bun raised her hand. I nodded in her direction and she hesitated before speaking.

"This doesn't match the expectation I had when I imagined what the clinical training would be like. Shouldn't we go back to the classroom and analyze what we just saw?"

" I don't really think we need to. The experience itself is what I wanted you to absorb. The feeling of having someone rely on you to get them through a situation that might kill them is massive, and you never get used to it." I walked over to the student and gently removed the pen from her hand. "Books and charts are really important in education, but they can't teach you what to feel." I capped her pen and slipped it into the front pocket of her lab coat. "Give that a rest for a while. This is the kind of information you can't capture on paper." She looked at me, and then a sly smile crept across her face.

"We'll see you Wednesday, Professor." A young man clapped me on the back, and then the group moved slowly toward the exits, discussing the day with one another. I stood in the fading sunlight, watching them go, and then I turned to walk up to the department.

"Knock, knock. Just checking in, bossman." I stood at the entrance of the manager's office and grinned as Tom pivoted his chair toward the door.

"Don't call me that, you ass. I wouldn't be sitting here if it wasn't for you," Tom said while shuffling a pile of papers on his desk.

"Does it feel funny to be sitting in the same place Todd was a few weeks ago?" I asked, leaning against the doorframe. "I know I'd be a little freaked out if I were in your place."

"It does feel odd to be in this room without any of the tension I used to feel. But I'm pretty sure I'll get used to it quick." Tom got up from his chair and walked over to where I was standing. "What about you? How's it feel to be back?"

"Surreal. I never thought this place would ever change but it has. In the space of two months, the whole landscape has changed. Todd is gone, and all of his lackeys followed suit."

"They were smart to do so. After the investigation, it would have been impossible for them to continue getting away with the shoddy work they were passing in. Most of them found jobs at the hospital across town, so at least they're still employed."

"I'm so glad we got Jordan to come back," I said, shifting my weight from foot to foot. "I knew he wouldn't be happy selling vents to managers."

"Nope. He couldn't wait to come back after he found out what was going on over here."

"Don't you people have anything better to do than gossip about me?" Jordan peeked his head around the corner.

"Ah, here he is now. Come, my bald friend, take a load off," Tom pulled out a chair for him next to the desk.

"No thanks. I just came in to verbally assault both of you before I go upstairs. I never pass up the chance to make trouble for the establishment." Jordan looked me over and clucked through his teeth. "And this is a sorry state of affairs, letting this person influence the minds of young people. Are you sure she knows what she's doing, chief?"

"I could say the same thing about you, moron. Maybe being a salesman has rotted your brain. Do you even know how to use your stethoscope, or did you forget where the lungs are?" I elbowed Jordan in the ribs and he doubled over laughing. "Maybe you should join my class on Wednesday and take a refresher course."

"I taught you everything you know. What could I possibly learn from you?" Jordan straightened up and yanked on my ponytail.

"How not to be an asshole? Oh, right, I forgot – you were born with the asshole gene."

"I don't have to sit here and take that abuse. I can get that at home." Jordan started walking down the hall toward the report room. He joined a few other therapists talking in the hall, right in front of the wall where the dreaded dry-erase board used to hang. That odious object had been the first thing Tom had removed after he was re-hired as the respiratory manager, and the difference it made was phenomenal. There were no more fights over assignments because Tom had devised a much simpler system for splitting up the workload, and it seemed to be effective.

I waved to Tom and walked down the hall to my own office, which was little more than a glorified closet. I had a battered desk and an old laptop computer, and that was it. My window couldn't be opened without a game of tug-of-war, and it looked out onto an alleyway. I sat down in the threadbare swivel chair and stared at the pile of evaluations I needed to fill out and began to shuffle through them.

"Knock, knock, " Amy rapped softly on my open door and leaned on the frame. "How was your first day?"

"It was very interesting. I don't think I've ever had so many people hang on my every word at the same time." Amy had also gone through some significant changes since the night on the helipad, and they were for the better. She had realized how little attention she had been paying to the department, and rectified that situation immediately after Todd left. Tom was mostly in charge now, but Amy made it a point to check in with every therapist on a weekly basis. These personal sessions had yielded some important information, but had also strengthened the relationship between management and therapists.

"I remember feeling that way a long time ago, but I got used to it and so will you. Is there anything you need to talk to me about before I leave for the weekend?"

"No, Amy, I'm good. But thanks for asking." I smiled as I gathered up the pile of papers I had been looking at. "I think I'll fill these out at home. So, any word on the Todd situation?" The morning after the helipad, Mr. Letiper had marched into the department and dealt with Todd personally. The meeting was held in Todd's office, and shouting could be heard through the closed door. Twenty minutes later, Todd emerged carrying his laptop and coat. He rushed to the elevators and left the building without saying a word to anyone. The next day, he sent a scathing resignation letter to the entire department and threatened a lawsuit for unfair working conditions. That had been nine weeks ago.

Amy smirked at me and moved aside as I walked into the hallway and locked my office door. "The last I heard, he was running a department – in Nebraska. Apparently that was where he grew up, and the hospital director is friends with his parents."

"Well, that's a lucky thing for him, isn't it? I'm just glad he's gone from here and we can finally get some good work done." I gave Amy a smile and put my hand on her shoulder. "I really appreciate all the support you've given me over the past few months, and I hope I can live up to your expectations."

"You already have. You were the catalyst for all of this change – if you hadn't taken a stand that night, this place would still be a dark hole." Amy reached out and hugged me. "I can't thank you enough for opening my eyes to all of this. I really had no idea what a miserable place this had become."

"Don't mention it. I'm just happy noone argues in the hall about their assignment anymore." Amy chuckled, and I could see that there was a new energy in her face that I hadn't seen there in years.

"OK, I'll see you on Monday for the meeting." Amy walked down the hall and popped her head into Tom's office. I walked past and pulled on my coat, pausing to look into the report room. There were eight therapists sitting at the long table, sharing information and jokes with one another. There was no fighting, no raised voices, and no snide comments. Jordan noticed me standing in the doorway and gave me a thumbs-up, followed by the bird. I grinned and shook my head – some things never change.

"Hey, here she is, the new instructor!" Thia hopped down from her bar stool and threw herself at me. I steadied myself against the wall and hugged her back, while Hannah stood by.

"You two look like you haven't seen each other in years. Get over it, OK Thia? She's my friend too, and I'm just as proud of her as you are." Hannah shoved Thia aside and wrapped her arms around me. Some of the other bar patrons had begun to stare, and I pried Hannah's arms off my neck.

"Come on, you guys. Let's sit down before we get kicked out." I led my friends to a table and draped my coat over a chair. "So how long have you two been here?"

"Since happy hour started. Half-price margaritas, how could we resist?" Thia slumped into the chair opposite mine and began slurping a drink. "Where have you been? We got drunk waiting for you."

"I had some things to wrap up in my new office before I left," I said, trying to get the attention of a waitress. "It is so bizarre to have my own office. Who would have thought?"

"US, you fool. You're finally getting the recognition you deserve after all your years of hard labor. You'll be able to teach those students things they'd never be able to get reading a book." Hannah shoved a handful of pretzels into her mouth and gestured wildly with her hands. "Those people are lucky you didn't just leave, and they know it."

I rested my chin in my hand and closed my eyes for a moment. After I had left the helipad that fateful night, I had driven straight home and met Sid. We talked over the situation for hours, and despite my worries about money Sid had convinced me that I did the right thing both for myself and the hospital. As I fell asleep in Sid's arms, I experienced a peace I hadn't felt in years. The uncertainty of my life faded away, and my dreams were filled with hope.

"Hey, you," Hannah poked me in the ribs. "What, are you tired already? The party's just getting started."

"Not tired, just thinking about everything that's happened. It's all changed so quickly - all the misery and fighting. And about a dozen therapists quit or got fired right after Todd left – the ones that everyone had a problem with. Now walking into that building is a joy, and I never thought that day would come."

"Well, it has and a lot of it has to do with you," Hannah said while squeezing my arm. "Aren't you proud of yourself?"

"I am, but it still seems like it's going to implode at any moment. It doesn't seem real." I reached over and grabbed a pretzel from the bowl on the table. " I hope it lasts, but what if the same thing happens again?"

"Then you'll fix it again," Thia said. "And now you have all the right people there to help you. Amy's on your side now, and Tom's there . . . hey, here he is!" Thia interrupted herself and skipped toward the door to greet Sid. Hannah squealed and followed suit, jumping up to hug him.

"Hey there," Sid said, grinning and disentangling himself from Hannah's octopus embrace. He leaned over and kissed me, his hair brushing my face. "So how was your first day as an instructor?"

"It was weird," I said, handing him a glass and pouring him a drink from the pitcher on the table. "All those kids looking up to me, hanging on my every word. I almost don't feel worthy."

"Well, that's asinine. If anyone can teach them the right way to do things, it's you," Sid said while sipping his drink. "You've got so much information in that noggin of yours, and it's not just medical jargon. You are going to reshape that place into a hospital that actually cares for people, not just how much their insurance will pay for."

I smiled and watched him trade quips with my friends and breathed in a huge breath; as I let it out, I thought about parents and how proud I hoped they would be of me. Happiness comes in small doses, and I'm willing to take them in any form. I sipped my coffee and leaned back in my chair, finally satisfied - for now.

Made in the USA
Middletown, DE
20 September 2023